I DO DANCE

Elizabeth Batory

TABB HOUSE
Padstow

First published 1996
Tabb House, 7 Church Street, Padstow,
Cornwall, PL28 8BG

ISBN 1 873951 02 7

British Library Cataloguing-in-Publication Data:
A catalogue record of this title is available from the British
Library.

Printed and bound by Short Run Press Ltd., Exeter

Elizabeth Batory is the author of

Come the Deep Water: Sea Stories

Contents

I Do Dance

``WHAT do they want me to do now?'' I wondered.

There where I stood, eyes level with the tops of my mother's legs I watched, horror-struck, as I saw in the vast space before me small figures knowing all about what they were supposed to be doing. Knowing it all. I feel my heart beating so fast, its thudding reaches up into my neck and makes my ears hot and red and confused. It means I don't hear properly when I'm like this. I hold Mummy's hand. She unravels me.

``Sarah, this is Miss Streete,'' she says.

A distant face smiles at me and says my name. My mother and she are talking. They are talking about me in secret and deciding what to do. They are plotting. I hear them making plans for me. It's something to do with dancing. So this is dancing? I know my mother said would I like to go dancing. I remember saying yes. I remember saying I thought I'd like it. I was wrong. Was this what I was saying yes to? She didn't say we were coming here today. She didn't say especially anything about today. These knowing and clever girls who have satin shoes on their feet and smart bands about their brows, are they dancing? No. There were to be . . . I remember now . . . there were to be long floating filmy dresses and a lot of hush. A sort of quiet stillness. Onto which I would float. And then I would find – like I might with swimming, or flying – because I'll do all these things one day

1

– I would find I would be dancing. And there would be sweet music and this floating. I'd be a lily, a water lily, white on a silver pond. And I'd float. That was the dancing I was talking about. But this . . . this looks like school. School in strange clothes, with none of the mothers kept out, because they are all here, buzzing, buzzing . . . loud like wasps round the marmalade jar when Daddy said . . . don't touch. But I did. And ow! But here they are buzzing and will sting me with the scorn in their proud faces. Because they will see I cannot do this.

I will not stand there with no satin slippers on and show all these people I cannot do any of this.

``Come on now, Sarah,'' says my mother.

Oh. The redness in my ears spreads to my face, and I feel that awful tight lump coming up, up into my throat. I know I will cry. I feel the shame, the embarrassment, the loss of dignity.

``Don't Mummy,'' I think desperately, ``don't make me seem foolish.'' The grey lady with the special sandals moves away in a cloud of perfume and all the little girls run to hold her hand. She smiles at them. Not at me. Not the outsider, hanging behind my mother, wishing to hide, wishing to die, wishing to be anywhere but in this world, in this place, here and now.

``Sarah,'' I hear the voice. There is anger on the edge of it, broken glass along the top of the wall. Her hands are tearing on it and she can't bear the world to see the blood running. I know it is because of me. My shame deepens. I glance tearfully at what is happening out there, all those miles away in that enchanted circle where all those clever dancing girls know exactly where to put their feet.

Then suddenly there is a chord.

The piano chings into life. I look out carefully, curiously, watching the lady who is watching everyone's feet, marking their movements in music.

She sees my astonished glare. I try to hide my rudeness. Before I can shuffle behind my mother's back, she gives me a smile.

Me? And I haven't even put my feet into a clever pattern.

Now they stand on their toes. Right on the top half of their feet. Cautiously I try my feet; behind Mummy's back I push my weight up and forwards. My feet bend quite happily.

The music trips around.

The greyish lady whirls by; her feet are marvellous. Big and strong and so confident in those sandals. I watch. I hold my breath. Can I launch myself? No, no. From here to there is so far. There is out and doing and managing. Here is disguised and hidden and secret. I will be a secret dancer. I will dance only alone and by night.

My hand reaches out, and the lady sees it, and holds me. Her hand is strong and cool, she smells sweet and her eyes are so soft.

``Run, run, run,'' she calls, ``lots of little steps. Oh, that is very good!''

Why, she means me!

Run, run, run I do. The wind takes my hair and the clouds lift me away and away and away. I float. I fly. We fold to the ground. We close up, tight little flowers, and as the great music swells we grow and grow. And if I watch the lady I can see what to do. And my body and my feet watch, too, and all parts of me do dance, do dance. I do dance.

Tending the Flame of Culture

A TENDER phrase of Schubert sounded over the radio. Miss Streete carefully re-arranged the posy ring of primroses. Early spring and clear sunlight hung in the air, laced with golden piano trills and perfumed with the sweetness of the primrose. The passage rang in her head and she hummed a little. ``Glissade, demi contretemps, assemblé . . . '' she muttered, seeing in her head the sparkling notes; spontaneous movements that the music was plucking idly from her bones.

She looked around for her book. There it lay on the sofa. She looked nervously at the book mark – it was only a third of the way through and tomorrow would be the meeting of the literary circle. She had only just been invited to join an earnest band of readers in her local village and, as she had only recently moved there, felt it would be a good way of getting to know some of the residents.

She wasn't entirely sure about the books – they seemed rather rude in places. They used the kind of language her mother would have labelled coarse. She prided herself that for a spinster she didn't really have spinsterish habits – but although she had waved goodbye to her virginity with abandon and relief in her early twenties, they still were not the kind of details she felt she needed. Her frissons arrived more often in the pump room at Bath where some neglected cousin in sprigged muslin unwittingly caught the eye of a droll roué ripe for reformation.

4

Still, needs must, and she abandoned the primroses to return to the book.

The sonata rose to stupendous heights. Miss Streete shivered, and couldn't help envisaging a *relevé* in fifth followed by a spectacular shoulder lift that swooned into a fish drive, held temporarily; she saw it all . . . in the mind's eye . . . that is the bliss of solitude.

The phone rang.

It was Jenny.

``Lara dear,'' she said, ``I've had a Mrs Hopkins on the phone; she wants to enrol Claire for tap and ballet. She is only three, and extremely talented.''

``They always are!'' Miss Streete observed.

She need not have made the reply; Jenny had already said it for her by a subtle alteration to the tone of her voice at the end of the sentence.

``And Annabel wondered if you would mind her missing one weekend at the end of May?''

``What for?''

``She has to see some relatives.''

That was always the trouble: leave Annabel in charge of one class whilst you snatch two minutes in the dentist's chair and she takes liberties. It isn't as though having a tooth crowned is any treat, either.

``I'll have not to mind,'' she said.

``I suppose so.''

``Any more messages?''

``No.''

``No problems?''

``No.''

``How's Jarvis?'' – Jarvis was Jenny's latest puppy.

``Fine.''

``Good. I'll see you Tuesday.''

``OK, then.''

```'Bye.''

```'Bye.''

The rolls of Schubert broke over Miss Streete like waves. The arabesque, supported, was slowly lowered into a breathtaking *penchée*. She braced her shoulders a little and smoothed down the page of the book in a determined manner.

The phone shattered the Schubert.

She answered.

It was Geoffrey. Geoffrey was Annabel's boyfriend – well, fiancé. Well – sometime fiancé – sometimes boyfriend – sometimes neither.

``Where's that bloody girl now?'' he demanded.

``Geoffrey,'' she remonstrated.

``C'mon then. Don't 'old out on me. I wanna know where she was last night.''

``Taking a class for me, if you must know.''

``Where the 'ell was you?''

``At the dentist,'' frostily.

``Right on?''

``Exactly.''

``You tell 'er to stop friggin' well mucking me about.''

``You tell her; you're of an age.''

Bang.

The receiver was replaced. Maybe these literary ladies were more in step with common parlance than she cared to admit.

After a while she put the book down in her lap and listened to the delicate ripples being etched on the air.

More steps and patterns and shapes surged through her.

Certainly the muse had descended. She made a bold decision. There will be another dancing display.

It was a couple of years since they did the last one. The

children all enjoyed it. The parents enjoyed it. All the little band of back stage helpers enjoyed it. In fact, everyone enjoyed it. As she recalled, everyone had had a good time – except – and she suddenly remembered – except her. That was it. For her it was an agony of nerves, weathering a welter of crises, lurching from horror to horror from the moment it was started until the gladsome moment when the last child had left the place of performance. Why on earth did she want to do it? Why on earth?

> Theirs not to reason why,
> Theirs but to do and die.

The same suicidal compulsion that urged the poor old six hundred into the valley of death assailed her. Nevertheless she should do it. Her mind raced.

A scenario was necessary. She cast her brain round the welter of myths and legends and fairy tales that were traditionally fair game. She found it. *The Nutcracker!* There was bound to be a piano version; she would mention it to Miss Pruett tomorrow. And phone Jenny about the idea later. In the meanwhile, perhaps she had better get back to the literary work.

She raised her eyebrows a little and settled back against the cushions on the sofa. The sunlight sought out the primroses and the Schubert achieved a final gentle plagal cadence.

She found her mind wandering.

The Schubert was replaced by a Haydn symphony. Haydn, she found, was even more conducive to mind-wandering than Schubert. Curious it was, she thought to herself, the position she occupied. Neither one thing nor the other. Take the literary ladies, for instance; they did not really count her as one of themselves. And it wasn't simply that she was not married. It was just that they didn't deal in the same currency. Her education had certainly brought her to the appreciation of the same things – it was, quite simply, that she did not earn nearly enough money to enjoy them. Her earnings really placed her in the category of some of her poorer pupils' parents, but she didn't belong there either – not in their eyes nor her own. It was a strange place to occupy – not quite in the same league as school teachers, closeted as she was in much more mystique. Her form of teaching was not amongst everyone's experience. It had any number of fearful pretensions. Pretensions to art and pretensions to gentility. She was regarded with fearful suspicion by the governing body of the church from whom she hired her hall. Had she been regularly worshipping the Golden Calf she couldn't engender much more disapproval. – She got up from the sofa. This kind of musing usually made her feel uncomfortable. She sought the solace of a cup of Earl Grey tea. She moved to the kitchen and reached for the kettle. – And yet she tried her utmost to bring a little culture and artistic appreciation to the children she taught. She genuinely wanted to lighten their world. She would urge them to listen to the delicacy of the *celesta* in the Dance of the Sugar Plum Fairy, she would talk of the noble Cossacks as she taught the Gopak.

``Wait for the oboe, children,'' she would call. ``That's when you start, when you hear the tune on the oboe.''

``You are Mars,'' she would thunder, ``the God of War – and you two are his charioteers – you find out their names and then tell them to me next week – and what those names mean in English.''

``Really Miss Streete,'' one of the mothers came up to her one day to say. ``Caroline's school teacher said that never before had she been asked to spell Eurydice!''

``I try,'' Miss Streete murmured to herself as she swilled the hot water round the teapot.

``The trouble is,'' she conceded, ``it seems to be expected that a degree of education means you will be part of a certain class, but even amongst the yuppies I am an object of suspicion, not simply because I belong to the *nouveaux pauvres* – many a teacher can claim that privilege – but because I show distressing symptoms of creativity.''

The surge of bergamot assailed her nostrils like a strong medicine.

She repaired to the lounge again.

She picked up the book.

``And if I don't watch it I will be used to sound off about the ladies' cherished offspring, if they think I have lowered my guard,'' she muttered to herself, and turned a few pages of the prescribed book.

``So what do I do?'' she asked herself, lapsing, and wishing Jenny would ring to say she'd lost Jarvis and could she come round to help her search for him.

``What do I do?''

She looked at the pale and decidedly rathe primroses. Their greeny bilious paleness quite unnerved her.

``Come now,'' she braced herself. ``You have anticipated it all already. You've done the hard bit – now just live through the scenario.''

``We are what we are,'' she said resignedly, and lifted the delicate bone-china tea cup to her lips, steadying the saucer beneath and gazing fondly at the posy of flowers. ``We can't do much about that, can we?''

Frostbite

SHE had arrived early. The hall was deserted; black shadows stained the floor. She dumped her bags and moved to the windows to pull the curtains. They let in a cold wave of early spring sunshine; harsh, cutting. The sky was pale green like a duck's egg. There had been frost in the night. She knew, because she had left her potted palm out in the rain the previous evening, forgotten it, and retrieved it this morning. She knew that damage had been done, but how extensive it was only time would tell. She was irritated with herself, having felt the complicity of guilt once she had acknowledged the damage. Plant slaughter, she thought to herself crossly, as she carried several cushions to the piano so that Miss Pruett might be more comfortable.

There was an overwhelming stillness now in this room. She sat in one corner, shoes changed, register open, open for business as it were, and there were no customers. Robbed of the other characters in this play she felt uncomfortable, bizarre even. Like travelling on a double decker bus in one's outfit for a fancy dress party. The hall throbbed like an unpregnant womb, waiting for an occupant to give it true purpose.

It had always amazed her that the church room in which she had had her first dancing lessons was also the place where she had attended Sunday School. On a Saturday the hall throbbed to the pounding of the piano and the footsteps of the children.

10

It smelt of coffee, cigarette smoke, perfume and ballet shoes. It was full of excitement and despair, strain and purple glory. Whereas on a Sunday it was hushed, sober and demure. There was pained nobility and reverential entreaty. The Margaret Tarrant pictures imparted the tone, she suspected: one of benevolent tranquillity. Mostly she enjoyed it; it smelt of wallflowers and candle wax and its music muted the wildness in one's spirit. But every now and again, perhaps when the wind was in the west, it incited her to overwhelming wickedness and she knocked the hymn book from her neighbour's hand and pretended to drop her penny for the collection, watching it roll towards the leader's ankles with guilty delight.

And yet the room was the same. It had once even been a ballet examination room. She had had to wait outside until the examiner's bell rang, and then with her report card in her hand she had presented herself at the examiner's desk, dropped a curtsey and waited for her instructions. And all the ghosts in the room, all its different *personae*, melted backwards and forwards into one another, while she waited, knees braced, feet in first, hair in bun, hair-netted and pink ribboned, for the ordeal.

And now this hall had seen generations of her pupils in various stages of their lessons with her. Had witnessed exam sessions, display rehearsals, private lessons, coaching lessons; had been empty, full, quiet, noisy; and times like now when she sat and wondered whether anyone would actually turn up for a lesson ever again. Then, like someone turning over in their sleep, or the tide turning, suddenly the school would be no more and all the pupils, teachers, mothers, fathers, pianists, assistants, hangers-on and camp-followers would fade away like a dream, only remembered in the shadows that ruined the floor and the walls.

*   *   *

The reverie was broken. The first mother arrived; manoeuvring a large push-chair through the door and with another child in tow, she steered her daughter into the hall. ``Are we the first?'' she asked.

``Looks like it,'' Miss Streete replied, getting up to bustle about while chasing out of her mind an intrusive pang of guilt about her palm.

It wasn't until Annabel arrived an hour later that she was able to get to the piano and have a chat with Miss Pruett. She had looked tired when she arrived, clasping her knitting and the daily paper. Miss Streete knew she wanted to be asked how she felt. Jenny took the signal of her moving to the piano to go into the kitchen and put the kettle on.

``You look tired, Clara,'' she said; ``how are you?''

``I'm all right really,'' Miss Pruett replied, resting her knitting in her lap and looking round at Annabel, waiting for a cue from her to start playing. ``The trouble is, though, I don't sleep so well at night these days.''

``Is there something troubling you?'' Miss Streete asked, looking at the gentle face with infinite concern, wondering why it was that the phrase `distressed gentlewoman' always came into her head when she looked at her pianist. After all, she was a working woman, an independent woman, a woman of her age and time. Except that she did not belong there, but more to a previous century when women gave teas, gave birth and were the backbone of England.

``I don't sleep, largely because my next door neighbours seem to be deeply into home improvements, and at all hours up to midnight I hear nothing but banging and tapping and scraping and sawing.''

``You should say something to them.''

``I keep meaning to and then I forget, and then by the time

it starts again I'm invariably in my nightie and looking quite unseemly, and haven't the effrontery to march to their front door and ask them to stop. Somehow being in one's night clothes robs you of all authority. I thought that when I was in hospital. It is an extremely clever move by the hospitals, you know, to strip you as soon as you go in. The staff immediately have the upper hand."

``If you're ready, Miss Pruett,'' Annabel called rather tersely.

``What was that, dear?'' Clara asked.

``Positions by *dégagé*; it's Grade One,'' Annabel replied.

``Set music?''

``Please.''

The chords sounded.

``I left my palm out overnight,'' confided Miss Streete, in a slightly hushed voice as though in the confessional.

``Oh dear; there was quite a frost last night wasn't there?''

``Yes. I had been seduced by the warmth yesterday, coupled with the rain; I thought that's just what the poor dear needed, cooped up all winter with all that dreadful central heating and the cats attacking the soil every now and again. I looked at the rain and I thought `That's what you need: the gentle fall of moisture on your leaves – That'll take you back to the jungles of Equatorial Africa, or wherever it is you came from.' ''

She sighed. The pupils turned at Annabel's command and faced the other way in the room and Annabel walked to the other end of the room to face them.

``And again on this side please,'' she said. ``Ready . . . and . . . '' she looked over at the piano to check that Miss Streete wasn't again distracting the attention of the pianist. ``And . . . ''

Miss Pruett was too much of a professional to be caught

twice; she looked mildly over her half-moon spectacles at
Annabel – all attention and anticipation. She depressed the
keys of the piano.

``They say it's a penalty of old age,'' Lara continued.

``What is?''

``Not being able to sleep.''

``Well, when it occurs naturally, I dare say,'' Miss Pruett
rejoined. ``But when it's simply because you happen to live
next door to Noah, it's nothing to do with you at all.''

``You think he's hard at it with the gopher wood then?''
Clara smiled.

``No one will believe you, you know,'' Lara added.

``No, not until the street is filled with a procession of
animals all lining up to go in, two by two.'' Miss Pruett
brought the piece to a close.

Miss Streete caught herself wondering when it was that
middle age slipped into old age. Perhaps it was when you
stopped thinking you had more time ahead of you than
behind you, when instead of saying `Oh well perhaps next
summer will be a better one,' when this summer had been a
wash-out of drizzle and driving, chilly winds, you thought
that this was yet another dreadful summer but maybe you
hadn't so many left. Or perhaps it was to do with attitude,
when you stopped being daring and adventurous; but she
knew that wasn't true because some of the young were by that
definition quite old. She looked round at the·children who
were now marking a *grands battements* exercise; she knew
among them who were the cautious and the coy, as well as
the risk takers. She knew she felt a youthful flame inside her
which the odd backache and muscular twinge denied, and
knew she was already at an age which she had designated old
when her grandmother, for instance, was that same age. She
glanced up at the row of mothers who were sitting watching

their daughters dance. Some were fighting rearguard actions, some with less success than others; others bubbled. True, clothing nowadays accented youthfulness and you could wear the badges until you were into your fifties, if you dared. But where was it you drew the line? When did you stop? Like her palm, there were parts that were fighting to stay green despite the ruin of the frost damage.

Jenny stopped her reverie by approaching with Annabel's and Miss Pruett's cups of tea.

``It's OK, Jenny,'' Lara said, ``I'm coming to the desk. I'll have mine over there with you. Anyway, I've got to sort out that leotard order and find those tapes.''

Miss Pruett picked up her knitting and thanked Jenny for the tea.

Annabel called ``The twelve-eight please . . . after two now.''

No sooner had Lara sat down than a mother approached her. A young mother. Hair a fizz of blonde bubbles, denim jacket and jeans.

``Can I have a word?'' she asked. Jenny disappeared with a child, a pair of ballet shoes and a length of ribbon.

``Of course, Mrs Lawson,'' she replied, and suddenly worried whether this meant trouble; sometimes `a word' meant a flea in the ear; a parental upbraiding that her teaching had failed the offspring's requirements in some way. Mentally she checked Diane's progress, but couldn't find anything but cause for praise. She indicated that they could go outside, out of earshot, if Mrs Lawson preferred. She looked round but, seeing that most of the other parents were sitting at some distance, decided the environs were private enough.

She came and stood on the other side of Miss Streete and looked down on her, face flushing a deeper shade of pink. Miss Streete guessed correctly that she was concealing herself from her child.

``I'd like a bill for Diane's fees,'' she said.

``Oh.'' said Miss Streete surprised, despite herself, ``but I'm sure you have paid for this term.''

``Can I have the totals then?''

``Oh,'' Miss Streete became calm efficiency. ``All right. Is that ballet, stage and tap?''

The mother nodded silently.

``And for the whole year?''

The mother was wordless. She swallowed. Miss Streete looked up into a face that was deluged by emotion.

``I need it for . . .'' She started again: ``My husband's traded me in for a younger model.'' She gulped. Lara stared, then checked herself.

`Younger?' she thought to herself, `you can't get much younger than . . . but – ' she exercised a mental shrug; she bit back an urge to say `good riddance'. The woman stumbled on, not noticing Lara's confusion in her own wash of emotion. ``I'm seeing the solicitor on Thursday,'' she said. ``I need to take some kind of statement with me . . . so we can work out . . . the money . . . '' Her voice became more and more incoherent and to her astonishment a hot tear fell on the back of her hand. Mrs Lawson angled and edged herself even more closely into the corner of the room, trying to hide herself, eyeing the dancing class covertly, terrified her daughter should see her in such distress. Her shoulders hung in a crescent under the waterfall of blond hair. She gulped.

``Here,'' said Miss Streete, ``sit down,'' and she indicated a chair, which the mother pulled over towards her.

A pair of track-suit trousers fell off the back and Miss Streete leant forward and picked them up. She started to fold them neatly. ``Don't worry,'' she said; ``I'll do what I can. – What else?''

``Well, if you could indicate the amount her shoes and leotards are, that would help as well,'' Mrs Lawson said.

Miss Streete turned in her chair and put the folded track-suit trousers on the table that served as a desk. She glanced up at Diane, who despite her straight back and attention to Annabel was tuned into every wavelength that had its source in her mother.

Jenny came in with a length of ribbon in her hands. ``Do you know,'' she said exasperatedly, ``they are still sending us lengths that are far too short to go round any but the slenderest ankles. We'd do better to buy it by the roll and cut it off and sell it ourselves. This'' – and she indicated the limp pink strands – ``is nothing but a waste.''

``Right,'' said Miss Streete, ``send it back and demand a refund, and order some of the roll instead. Keep a check of the price; if they refuse a refund we'll not stump up, at the next bill.''

She felt grateful to get her teeth into something, something she could be tough and harsh with, anything to cut free from the distress that was emanating from the woman next to her. She knew what else would happen, because she had seen it all before. She knew Diane was going to have a bad time. That she'd probably under-achieve in her next couple of exams in which she had stood a good chance of being highly commended. She would undergo an overwhelming crisis of confidence from which she would emerge either tougher and better prepared for whatever else life would throw at her, or forever damaged and never entirely healed. But you never entirely knew which. Something similar was true of the mother. Something also had bitten into the green life of her, cut into the quick and vital centre of her, causing unspeakable and irreparable damage. Failed self-regard was as vicious as frost, Lara knew.

Jenny looked at Miss Streete and then across at Mrs Lawson. Lara explained the situation as dryly as she could.

``Oh we'll make it as much as we can,'' said Jenny cheerfully, ``every last charge, including several lengths of ribbon.'' And she laughed.

Mrs Lawson managed a smile.

``Would you like a cup of tea?'' Lara asked.

Mrs Lawson nodded, gradually regaining control. ``If it's not too much bother.''

``None at all,'' said Jenny and disappeared into the kitchen.

``I'll have the bill ready by Monday,'' Lara said. ``Is that all right? You can pick it up after Diane's tap lesson.''

``Fine,'' nodded the mother and lowered her defeated eyes to her lap. Then she looked up under her eyelids at her daughter. Diane met her gaze and gave her a nervous smile and let her eyes travel to Miss Streete. She smiled encouragement and was relieved to see, just by the minutest fraction, Diane's chin rise and her chest lift, and then she refocused her attention and was back in Annabel's class again.

``She's doing very well, you know,'' Lara said, by way of encouragement.

``It's what keeps me going, really,'' Mrs Lawson confirmed, and looked up gratefully as Jenny put a mug of tea in her hand. Like a mist clearing, a sharper light shone in her eyes.

Miss Streete heard the music for the curtsey. ``I'm teaching the next class,'' she said. ``I'll have it all ready for you Monday. Good luck for Thursday and if there's anything else . . . '' she left the sentence unfinished.

Mrs Lawson nodded and gulped, but this time it was tea in her throat, not a lump.

Annabel put the grade book in her hand as they passed each other. She was carrying her cup of tea. ``I'm going to go and gossip in a distracting way to the pianist now,'' she said provocatively.

``Carry on,'' said Miss Streete, ``but she will blame you if she drops a stitch, you know.''

``Yes, I know,'' she said. ``– No, actually, I'm going to look for those tapes; I don't suppose you found them?'' She looked at Miss Streete slightly accusingly.

``No I didn't; slight crisis at Base Camp. Be nice to Mrs Lawson . . . Jenny'll explain.''

She caught Miss Pruett's eye and cast her own to heaven.

By the end of the morning, in between exercises, classes, breaks natural and unnatural, Miss Pruett was fully cognizant of the situation.

``A lovely young girl like that,'' she said, over and over again, and ``She's so young . . . '' and she'd shake her head and knit one, purl one with deft determination.

The hall was empty again. Only Miss Streete and Miss Pruett remained. All the sounds and sighs had fled, and hung now like cobwebs somewhere high on the walls near the ceiling.

``Oh well,'' Miss Streete said, ``home to see how the palm is making out.''

``I don't know,'' said Miss Pruett; ``it's the silly and careless way that damage is done that depresses me.''

``Maybe it's surviving the damage that's really the important thing, though,'' Miss Streete mused, ``and ageing an inability or refusal to survive the damage.''

``In which case we would all live for ever,'' Miss Pruett said.

``You would, you mean,'' Lara laughed; ``but others may decide that it's no longer worth it. I'll let you know if I've got a senile palm, next week.''

``And I'll let you know if you have a senile pianist,'' Miss Pruett rejoined.

Bewitched

I CAN't handle what the world throws at me – jostled here, squashed and hot at the back of this hall – walked here protesting, with my sister in her push-chair – by Mummy – from school. Already the hall is full; lots of faces, lots of coats, lots of bodies, puffing and bubbling on the canvas-seated chairs. The hall smells of dust and cloth and perfume, custard tarts, and rubber and the late afternoon sunshine. It slants across the room in chalky strands. We need a place with the push-chair close; Mummy wants it close and safe and my sister close and safe; so we have to move further and further into the darker recesses of the hall, until we are right at the back, by the wall – the wall festooned with three red fire buckets. She has found a table to put me on. ``You'll be safe there; I'm only just down here,'' – and herself sitting a little distance away.

Some of my school friends join me. We are huddled and waiting and jabbering. They, too, are to watch but I'm still bewildered. I'm told it's the summer concert – but what is that? My friends all seem to know. Mummy knows, but I don't know. I think it is something to see, because we are going to watch; everyone is facing the curtains – the drawn curtains – dusty and heavy with mystery, at one end. I hide my ignorance and pull again at my white cotton socks, wet my finger with spit and make the brown leather of my sandals all shiny again. I am getting hotter and hotter; the conversation churns around me, boiling, rupturing, engulfing. Suddenly I'm cross – I don't want to be here – I'm pushed by more of my school-mates crowding into this vantage point on the table and suddenly Bang! – my head sounds against the red metal of the fire bucket. OW! Hot tears blink and swim and sting my eyes. I won't cry – I won't – but holding it back – holding it back – the wave of disgrace and humiliation brings that oh, so familiar uncomfortable lump into my throat. I hide my face and misery by hanging my head and start picking at the scab on my knee – the're always scabs on my knees and it's usually a slap and a call – Don't pick them! – but Mummy can't see; she's leaning over Celia and wiping her nose. I frown furiously at my knees and then feel a tear escape; it's hot and trickles down my cheek. I put out my tongue to catch it and sip – warm and salty. I want to be away from here.

Were I at home I could have pushed through the hole in the fence in the back of the garden and erupted into the raucous golden cornfield. I could listen to the earth breathing as a breeze ruffles the swaying grain and watch the grasshoppers spring away at my approach. The meadow browns would scatter over the rusty red dock plants and I'd find the stream, and plundering this other world, this other kingdom, I'd feel it breathe me in and absorb me and I'd return safe, safe again to the parenting elements.

A ripple runs through the murmuring in the hall, a bubbling wave of excitement; it wafts through and back to me, delivering a glancing blow, lifting my chin and my gaze – to the curtains. They are bruised with lights, dusted now in peach and blue. Then the knife of the guillotine falls, and silence heavy as death seizes us all. My breath ceases. The curtains divide. They pull apart. And there, swamped in gold, four girls, limbs of glass, delicate as the veins in the dragonfly's wings, wrapped in fragments of the rose-misty dawn, solemnly move in rapturous trance. I am transfixed. I am pierced to the heart. It is another world. I have felt other worlds, I have dreamt other worlds; flowers and places have shown me them and words have painted pictures – but now I see it with my own eyes. It lives and breathes in front of me. Oh, with what sorrow does it end – and my hand claps, my fierce and sweaty claps are saying more, more, more, give me more. And as though that magic works, obligingly if jerkily the curtains re-open. And a little boy, dressed as a cat, sings and recites and I wonder at his skill. The joy fills my eyes with sparkling stars, the excitement seizes my body and I tauten; it makes me babble and babble between acts to my friends – and I am so pleased with Mummy to have brought us here.

And the wildness of the waves of the tossed sheeting, and the glamour of the diamonds in the crowns, the richness of the robes, the utter splendour of it all! How drab the cream paint on the brickwork walls, the butt-end in the sand in the fire bucket, the splintered and sundered edge to the table. How stark and dry and difficult the schoolroom, parental reprimand, the urge to duty and the necessary. How fierce the stings of my school-mates' derision, the sickening sudden sundering of friendships, the violent fights, jealousies and rivalries; the whole ruck and tumble of home, the street and playground – but here – here I can hide – I can hide and be lost by looking at the magic square, falling into it and submerging myself in its enchantment.

Charm upon charm – and I have become removed and drunk with delight – and then at yet another parting and another revelation, amongst a group of fairies is Wendy. Wendy! from my school. From our school. Someone I know. And Wendy is translated. She is that fairy creature – and a compulsion, the greatest wish, the deepest need, the fiercest desire is born. I watch Wendy with greedy eyes. I wish it to be me. I know I cannot just watch this world – oh no – no, I need to be in it – to be of it. Just as something of me belongs to the woodland, the shore, the cornfield, so something else needs to fly home here, roost, return.

My needy gaze is interrupted. It's Mummy, and although she's partially apologetic I know she's insisting we go. She says it's all gone on too long and we must return home. Gone on too long? Oh, it's not gone on long enough. I want more of it – and more. I plead. I yearn. But she's insistent. The more petulant I am the harder her eyes become, and the severer the lines of her mouth. In the end she takes my arm and I am hauled away from the dangerous sea of enchantment. Eyes still on the stage, I am trailed from the hall. But it's too late – too late – the spell has been cast and I have been caught for ever.

Mrs Makepeace

MRS Makepeace usually loitered a moment or two by the door before she departed. The moment of separation was obviously more painful for her than it was for her daughter. Liane looked on apprehensively at her mother's discomfort. Then, once the large shape had withdrawn, she smiled and skipped and ran to join in with her friends. Jenny and Lara would watch this ritual ruefully from the side lines.

Sometimes Mrs Makepeace came up to Miss Streete to tell her of some infirmity from which her offspring was momentarily suffering. She had a confidential tone, pale skin and a chin densely populated with white facial down. It was a gentle, patient face, the face that belonged to someone who could if demanded wait uncomplaining for a long, long time. Hers was the face of tea shops, bus queues and hotel foyers.

What was a surprise was the smallness and delicacy of Liane. How this sturdy, stocky, if upright lady had given birth to such a frail child was a constant surprise to Lara. Furthermore, Liane was graceful and adept and quick mentally and physically.

Mrs Makepeace gave Liane another last look, smiled indulgently and set sail into the spring sunshine. She waddled patiently from the hall whilst the notes of the melody from Miss Pruett's piano ran mistily through her brain. She had a lot to keep her busy.

Although Liane and her father were all of her domestic

responsibilities she also had her role in the local school 7–
Liane's school – to occupy her. Another school bazaar was
imminent and she had more felt and polyfoam chips to
purchase if she was going to make enough cuddly toys for the
stall that she usually manned. And then there would be the
speciality bear for the raffle. Apart from her toy-making role
she had made herself virtually indispensable in other ways –
she coached the junior recorders and helped daily in the
school library where her innate sense of order was invaluable.

She winced a little as she crossed the road. She wondered
what the school would do without her once Liane left.
Imperceptibly, she had just got more and more involved. It
was a creeping association: it had started with an offer of help
one Christmas when the nativity play had demanded some
backstage helpers and had gradually moved into a wordless
interdependence.

In the meanwhile Liane stretched and tensed her little
muscles and ordered her feet to follow the complex pattern of
the dance.

Miss Streete smiled at her. ``That's lovely! Well done,
Liane,'' she said.

Liane blushed furiously.

Lara moved over to Miss Pruett and, resting her hand
along the top of the piano, said ``She's lovely, isn't she?''

``Which one?'' asked Miss Pruett, looking carefully over
the top of her half glasses.

``Liane Makepeace,'' Lara replied. ``She seems to know
what to do instinctively.''

``Yes, it's funny isn't it?'' replied Miss Pruett. ``They seem
to be born understanding. No amount of instruction, despite
their passion to learn, is going to replace or make up for . . .
what is it? . . . Instinct . . . I suppose.'' She glanced back from
Liane to the music.

Lara had turned the page. ``*Pas de chat,*'' she indicated.

Miss Pruett lifted her chin and looked at the top of the page.

As the children were dancing round the room, she flicked her eyes from them to the music. Then at Miss Streete's instigation she enticed them to movement with a Brahms waltz. Lara cast her appraising glance over them. Liane had moved from the far corner of the room into the centre; she caught Lara's smile and then immediately averted her gaze. But at the same moment a new dignity surged into her limbs and she commanded more attention.

``Mind you,'' said Miss Pruett, glancing back to the keyboard and then up at Lara again, ``she's one that thrives on encouragement.'

``Don't we all?'' murmured Miss Streete.

On Monday morning Mrs Makepeace sat at the desk of the school library, calmly resorting the tickets that had been left in a careless muddle on Friday, her afternoon off. She smiled a little to herself, an action that revealed two dimples in her otherwise heavy face, and hummed a little, recognising the tune as the one she had heard at the dancing school. She heard a sound and looked up. Miss Rivett, the deputy head, had come into the library and was looking quickly along the shelves for a book.

She gave her a quick smile. ``Can I help you find anything?'' she asked.

``No. I know what I'm looking for, thank you,'' came the slightly muffled reply; in stooping, Miss Rivett found her breathing somewhat restricted.

Mrs Makepeace regarded her bowed blonde head with a feeling akin to maternal pity. She knew how hard teachers worked, how difficult their lives were. Heaven knew, she found her weekly half hour with the first year recorders more than enough. And she also knew what some of them had done for Liane, who had been a lonely, only child who at first had found school particularly unnerving. Had it not been for the gentle motherly reassurance given to her by her reception class teacher she might well have gone under. And there had been Miss Whatmough who had taken such pains with her fractions and Mr Thomas who had encouraged her to swim. Even outside school Liane had prospered under the indulgent eye of Mrs Bracey, her piano teacher, and Miss Streete, her ballet teacher. Mrs Makepeace could not think more highly of any profession. To her, teachers were a blessed breed. Blessed with a vocation which she earnestly wished she possessed. Her way of expressing thanks was through the time and labour she gave back to the school. And in this she was unstinting. She was another pair of eyes on a school trip, she was another pair of hands at the PTA cheese and wine, she swung along at the upper school leavers' disco, she donated the teachers boxes of biscuits to lift their flagging spirits, she gave them discount on goods from the cosmetic agency she ran as a little sideline.

Unable to help Miss Rivett with her search for a book, she asked, ``Have you enough parents for the farm visit on Tuesday?'' How she knew about the farm visit on Tuesday was not questioned; her omniscience went without saying.

``Yes thank you,'' said Miss Rivett, somewhat peremptorily and not bothering to unstoop.

``Did you enjoy the disco on Thursday?'' Mrs Makepeace continued, full of good humour. ``I think the children really enjoyed themselves.''

Miss Rivett was silent, her short fingers still running swiftly across the book spines. Then she uncoiled, and pulled herself up on her high heels. She shot Mrs Makepeace a glacial winter-blue smile and removed herself from the library.

Miss Rivett was a woman with a mission. She knew, when she first glimpsed this school, frowning under its low roof, squatting defensively in its hollow of rolling playing fields, that it was to be here that she would make her mark. When her appointment as deputy head was duly signed and sealed her zeal was confirmed. Her rise through the ranks of teachers had been meteoric, and usefully advantaged by close liaisons with various members of the educational hierarchy, with one of whom she now lived. Prudence and the enhancement of career prospects suggested that they should legalise the union and that was safely booked to be done the forthcoming Easter.

Now it was time to make her bid for a headship and here was the means of making her mark. The school was ripe for enhancement; its reputation and hers. She unfurled her colours, crouching over the desk of an office area she had created for herself at the back of the old school canteen. There she drew up rotas and lists, time-tables and schemes of work. The staff here had had it too easy for too long; now they were going to have to earn every last penny of their money to warrant those ridiculously long holidays the duration of which she mostly suffered in unutterable boredom.

She filed, she classified, she threw out old schemes and introduced new schemes. She reorganised time-tables, she terminated traditions, she instituted new habits.

Eventually the more hectored, the least favoured members of staff retired, mortally wounded, and sought employment elsewhere. But, as she said to the slightly punch-drunk headmaster, ``You can't make an omelette without breaking eggs.'' He, a man acutely embarrassed by his own intellectual shortcomings and absence of cultural acumen, had long since retired to the touch-line where he was both unwilling and unable to intervene.

When a particularly lachrymose probationer finally lost confidence and left the profession after only six months, she was said to have remarked tartly ``If you don't like the heat, you should stay out of the kitchen,'' seemingly unmindful of who was playing the role of stoker.

The one person whom she appeared not to have shaken was Mrs Makepeace. Undeterred, she continued her loyal support, oblivious of the unpleasant remarks that were said behind her back or behind the closed staff room door. And Liane progressed slowly but inexorably through the school. Diligent and persevering, displaying much of the tenacity of her mother, she passed exams in both piano playing and ballet. However, lest it might appear that she might be favoured, somehow, as her mother's daughter, and Miss Rivett thereby discountenanced, she was rarely allowed a public display of her talents in school activities.

``You'll never guess what she is wearing today!'' Miss Rivett said to a colleague as she moved into the staff room. ``Some pale green confection with every last accessory matching. She looks like the iceberg that finished the *Titanic*.''

``It could be one of her few pleasures, dressing up to come here looking smart,'' suggested a younger staff member, who was contradicted by a withering glance.

``She means well,'' ventured the school secretary.

``She's an unmitigated nuisance,'' replied Miss Rivett, pulling her bread roll apart with quick predatory fingers and putting pills of bread in her mouth in a gobbling manner. ``She'd be in here for two pins,'' she continued. ``That's always been her ambition – to get her nose into running the affairs of the school.''

``But they're not really run from in here anyway, are they?'' suggested a second-year teacher, searching in her basket for some work cards and probably envisioning the desk at the back of the canteen. Not finding them, she walked back from the staff room to the classroom where she must have left them on her desk. On the way she passed through the hall, where the benign bulk of Mrs Makepeace sat at the piano in a miasma of perfume and rippling chords. A semi-circle of recorder players clustered in an untidy arc behind her and whistled and blew an approximation of the melody of `The Snowman'. She took in the pale jade shoes, the matching earrings and was touched. Surely, those that cared so much could not be construed as dangerous, she wondered. And then she remembered Miss Rivett and shuddered – for perhaps there were cases where they could.

Entering the classroom, she saw Liane and a group of friends playing a fortune-telling game. She had an idea.

Mrs Makepeace had more reason to engage Miss Streete's sympathetic ear next Saturday morning.

``Miss Dunne has asked Liane to do a butterfly dance at the end of term concert and wondered whether you would mind giving her a few steps.''

``Not at all, if you can find out what music she is dancing to,'' said Lara, delighted to have the opportunity to see what Liane could do if stretched and if in addition she could have her on her own for a few sessions.

``I asked, and she said she's put it on cassette for you if you were happy about that.''

``Fine,'' said Miss Streete, and on subsequent Thursdays, while Annabel took the preliminary stage class, she coached Liane.

Mrs Makepeace wondered whether Miss Pruett, Jenny and Lara would like to watch the performance. They agreed readily. As Lara said to Jenny, she always liked the opportunity to nose at other people's performances, particularly if she found some ideas to filch.

``And thank you for lending her the costume,'' confided Mrs Makepeace.

``Let her wear it for the last rehearsal,'' suggested Lara. ``That way she'll get used to dancing in it.''

That Thursday she arrived to find Jenny and Mrs Makepeace struggling with a pair of butterfly wings and antennae, whilst Liane squirmed under their deft manipulation.

``It has to be really tight here,'' explained Jenny, ``if the wings are going to stand away from the body.''

Mrs Makepeace looked alarmed.

Lara laughed. ``Oh, we reckon to restrict bust development by at least five years with all the girls that have been our butterflies,'' she said.

``Well, exactly,'' said Mrs Makepeace.

``But Jenny does know what she is doing – she's a real dab hand,'' she reassured Mrs Makepeace.

Liane stepped back. The three women scrutinised the end product.

``Give us a flit round the room, then,'' said Jenny.

Liane twirled away, suddenly light and airborne. She caught a glimpse of herself in the mirror as she passed it and smiled at her reflection.

``It looks really good, doesn't it, Mum?'' she called.

``Oh yes,'' agreed Mrs Makepeace. ``Thanks, Miss Streete,'' she added. ``I could never have got it to look like that.''

``Oh, that's fine,'' said Lara; ``just part of our vast wardrobe. You may as well borrow it and make good use of it,'' and her eyes strayed to where Liane was still fluttering round the room, synchronising the movements of her body so that the wings moved with her.

Miss Streete always felt slightly strange when she ventured

over the threshold of a school. She had arranged to meet
Jenny and Miss Pruett there, as she needed to pop home after
the classes had ended. She felt somehow part of the
establishment and yet at the same time very displaced.
Perhaps it was because she taught quite a number of the
children who went to this school, perhaps it was because she
was in the same line of business or perhaps it was because on
occasion she had been called in to provide steps, ideas or
dances for this or that production over the years. Some of the
staff were once familiar to her, but now no longer. There
seemed a lot more new faces. She was relieved and pleased
when the school secretary greeted her warmly.

As she walked down the corridors she couldn't help
sliding back into the memories of her own first school. The
smells were so familiar, as was the sight of shoebags hanging
on pegs and art work ornamenting the walls.

Even if she hadn't remembered the way to the school hall
she could have found it by following the sound that emanated
from it. A warm dense brown sound of adult voices and
excited children. But before she got there the tap of high heels
behind her made her turn round. Miss Rivett was gaining on
her in a meaningful manner, her arms full of books of music.
She paused and Miss Rivett moved past her.

Then she stopped and turned and regarded her. ``Can I
help you?'' she asked, giving Lara her icy smile.

``Oh no, it's all right, thank you,'' said Lara. ``I know
where I'm going.''

``Oh good,'' replied the other, suddenly giving Lara the
feeling that it was just as well for her that she did. She turned
and carried on.

A teacher was waiting by the door. ``Oh you've got the
music,'' she said in a slightly flustered voice to Miss Rivett. ``I
was just coming to get it.''

``Well, you don't have to now, do you?'' replied Miss Rivett curtly, ``as I've got it here.''

``Thanks,'' said the other one and looked abashed.

She was swept by a wave of cool appraisal, weighed in the balance yet again and found wanting. Lara looked away to cover her embarrassment and to avoid hurting the other one's feelings. Miss Rivett disappeared into the hole of noise that was the hall. Before Lara could follow her she saw Jenny push her way out.

``Ah, thank goodness you're here,'' she said, giving Lara her serious look.

``Anything the matter?'' asked Lara quickly, knowing full well that there was.

``You'd better come with me, I think,'' said Jenny. And then added ``It's OK, Clara will keep our seats.''

``What's up?'' asked Lara.

``Well,'' said Jenny, as she led the way down a corridor and round a corner and out of earshot of the hall. ``I don't know all of the story, but I gather there was a bit of a kerfuffle at the rehearsal.''

``What kind of a kerfuffle?'' asked Lara.

``Aah, well now you're asking,'' said Jenny. ``The truth is, I don't really know, but it transpired that during the rehearsal words were exchanged between Miss Rivett and Mrs Makepeace, the upshot of which is Mrs Makepeace has been asked to remain off the school premises.''

``Well, not so she can't see her child perform, surely?'' asked Lara.

``No, no, she's in there at the moment.''

``Well, then, she is allowed on the premises.''

``Only to see the performances but not afterwards.''

Lara was still mystified, until Jenny explained to her the role that Mrs Makepeace had held in the school since Liane had started at the reception class almost six years ago. Lara started to get the picture.

``Was that Miss Rivett who I saw just as you came out of the hall?'' she asked.

``Yes,'' confirmed Jenny.

``Aah!'' said Miss Streete, putting more of the pieces of the picture in place. ``But . . . why?'' she began.

``Liane,'' explained Jenny. And they passed a large window now ultramarine with the night sky behind it, and turned sharply right and entered a brightly lit classroom.

Miss Dunne saw them approach and came up to them. She waved aside several clamouring, highly excited be-costumed children. ``I must say thank you first of all for lending us the costume,'' she said, ``and for teaching Liane such a lovely dance.''

``Oh any time,'' said Lara. `` – Now what's the matter?''

``Well, I can hardly say that I don't know,'' replied Miss Dunne, her slightly pink face becoming even pinker, ``and it would be unprofessional for me to say too much; but there was a bit of bother during the rehearsal.''

Lara waited, and Jenny who never knew how to avoid such things started absent-mindedly zipping rabbits into their costumes and pinning rabbit ears into place with hair clips.

``I'm not taking sides, you understand,'' continued Miss Dunne, ``and we are all under considerable strain at the moment, not just putting on the end of term show, you realise, but'' – and Miss Streete could hear her putting the words in italics – ``*in the profession*. And the emphasis is on profession. Our deputy head is very concerned that everything at the school should be as professional as possible . . . and that sometimes means doing away with unprofessional – if well-meaning – assistance!''

Miss Streete watched Jenny tweak a pair of plaits over a

child's head and deftly place a head-dress over the crown. She wondered briefly and bleakly what standing Jenny would have in Miss Rivett's eyes.

``So what can I do to help?'' she asked.

Miss Dunne looked relieved that she was not being asked to explain more. She swung her fair head round and looked round the room. ``Where's Liane?'' she asked a red-haired boy whose two new front teeth more than amply justified his role as a rodent.

``In the art room,'' he replied.

``Go and have a few words with her,'' Miss Dunne beseeched. ``She says she can't dance.''

``How bad was it?'' Lara asked, looking Miss Dunne straight in the eye. ``I mean did Liane know?''

``Oh yes,'' Miss Dunne nodded. ``I gather everyone knew. Voices were raised. We all get awfully worked up at the end of term you know . . . it's such a pity.''

Lara looked at her. She suddenly seemed pathetically young. But it occurred to her in the words of the sage that if she wasn't part of the solution then she too was part of the problem. But then what kind of a life does anyone make for themselves when they start boat-rocking? She probably wanted a couple of years in this job before settling down and starting a family with some earnest young man. She didn't want job hunting and climbing career ladders, she wanted a peaceful life. And she was prepared to let the ladder-climbers bruise what knuckles they would. And gather up a few other casualties en route. *Tant pis.*

``Can we have a few uninterrupted moments then?'' asked Miss Streete.

``Yup,'' replied Miss Dunne, burying her shamed face in a blond helmet of hair as she stooped down and adjusted the horse's rather lopsided hoofs.

``I'll keep all the kids out of there. – Our play is in about a quarter of an hour,'' she added in a loud stage whisper to Lara.

Jenny turned to her. ``I'll get back and tell Clara I've seen you,'' she said.

Miss Streete found the forlorn butterfly sitting dejectedly in the corner of the art bay. All around her a sea of *papier mâché* masks leered down at her, their lurid painted faces a kind of silent mockery. Lara looked at the tear-stained face.

``Miss Streete,'' the child said in alarm as she looked up and saw Lara looking at her. ``What are you doing here?''

``What are *you* doing here?'' Lara replied.

``I just . . . I just . . . oh, Miss Streete, it was so awful!''

``I expect it was,'' was all Lara could think of saying. The child sobbed and her thin body convulsed and squirmed with the agony of recollection and humiliation.

``I always knew Miss Rivett. . .'' and here she stopped again, and then swallowed and lifted her pale face and suddenly looked out of the window. It was as though she was lost in a dream. Lara waited. Then suddenly Liane's tears started trickling down her face again. Lara felt for a handkerchief in her pocket, could only find some tissue and this she handed to Liane.

``And Mummy . . . '' and she cried again.

Slowly the sobs stopped and she shuddered suddenly to a halt.

``And all the time we were getting ready to go out . . . '' she went on in a strange bleak little voice, ``Mummy . . . '' and she started crying again.

Lara knelt down beside her and put her arm round her. ``Did this happen in front of all the children?'' she asked.

``Oh no,'' said Liane in a rush. ``No; only I was there then, and even I didn't really know . . . that . . . but . . . Mummy's

face . . . and I . . . well; she told me afterwards what it
meant.''

``Right,'' said Miss Streete, suddenly business-like again.
``And if they've heard about it they'll forget. You know? In
schools and places people don't have very long memories.''

``It'll take such a lot of forgetting,'' said Liane; ``she's been
here as long as I have.''

``But you have the perfect means of helping people
forget,'' said Lara, suddenly realising she had what she
needed now.

``Have I?'' asked Liane, ingenuously.

``Yes,'' said Lara with deep conviction. ``What you can do
is to make everyone remember the concert and your butterfly
dance. They will forget the rehearsal. And later on when
people say `Oh, doesn't Liane Makepeace go to that school?'
instead of people saying `Oh yes, and didn't her mother run
the library' . . . or whatever it is they might remember your
mum doing, they will say, `and do you remember that was
the first place we saw her dance, when she did that butterfly
dance at the end of term concert?''

``They won't say that,'' said Liane, suddenly flattered and
petulant.

``Won't they?''

``No.''

``Well then, it's up to you to make them.''

Liane was silent.

Lara added ``You could, couldn't you? You know you
could.'' She stood up, wincing slightly at the pain in her knee,
and looked down at the small figure, remembering suddenly
the conviction that she once had running through her like
quicksilver in her veins, when she moved like that across the
stage, commanding every attention and knowing she was
getting it. She fished another tissue from her pocket and lifted

the face under the chin and wiped the eyes. The eyes looked
back, no longer melancholy but burning with an elfin glow.

``Just you go and do it. I shall be watching.'' And with that
Lara departed.

As she passed Miss Dunne she said quickly and quietly
``You've got your butterfly!''

And Liane did it, just as Lara knew she could. Jenny, Miss
Pruett and she exchanged knowing smiles. The audience
sensed that something very special was unfolding in front of
them. The teachers, impotent in all but their sympathy,
watched and applauded, enraptured and delighted. Mrs
Makepeace watched and was transported, forgot her hurt and
unhappiness, if only temporarily.

Miss Rivett was delighted with the applause, if only
because it meant the successful completion of yet another
school enterprise. She couldn't really understand what all the
fuss was about Liane Makepeace's dance; after all a dance was
just a dance, wasn't it? She reminded herself to drop that
application form for the headship at St Mary's into the post on
the way home.

Mrs Makepeace removed Liane's wings, looking at them
again, wondering how they were made. She thought that she
could probably manage something like them, if required, and
wondered whether Miss Streete would like another helping
hand to add to Jenny's when it came to getting together the
costumes for her next show. She had an intuition that dancing
was going to occupy a large proportion of her life and Liane's
in the future.

She smiled at Liane. ``You were wonderful, Liane,'' she
said, bursting with maternal pride and happiness. ``You were
just like a beautiful butterfly.''

``I know,'' said Liane.

Selling The Dream

ANNABEL pushed out of the swing doors; the clock said a quarter to one. Miss Streete glanced at it, wishing it didn't. She knew Annabel knew she knew and, together, they had exchanged another message.

As she called the next class of children to come into the hall and get themselves ready for the class she glanced out of the window. She saw Annabel's spring-like body walking quickly to her little red Fiat Uno. She noted the pony tail, the track-suited legs, the strange swing that propels a dancer's legs forwards from the hips and the big bag like a roll of laundry over her shoulders: all badges and all needed. For Annabel was a dancer who rarely danced and, like an actress who didn't act or a singer who didn't sing, she found if she wasn't actually engaged in her occupation, it was dangerously easy to lose hold of her identity. She'd opted for the compromise, she taught dancing. And whenever people asked her what she did she would say ``Oh, I teach dancing,'' lightly, carelessly, and then look into the face of the questioner, watching the blink of scorn or the iris-clouding knowledge of complicity, the overpowering, if unspoken phrase of condemnation: those that can, do; those that can't, teach. But Annabel was still trying to do, and yesterday had been at The Palace, at an open audition for chorus dancers in a new Lloyd Webber musical.

Pamela came up to her. ``Can you fasten my ribbons, Miss

Streete?'' she asked. ``Daddy did them, and they are very uncomfortable.''

She looked down at Pamela's skinny legs, the scabby knees, and the pulled-up socks. The child was cross-gartered to mid-calf and a large lop-sided bow hovered on her shin. She laughed.

``Daddy hasn't got the hang of these, has he?'' she said, and she looked up at the girl, who was looking round at her classmates with glassy blue eyes.

Two girls were taking it in turns to jump from the chairs they used as a barre.

``Stop doing that Tarzan act, Tracey,'' she called. ``And Jane, take off all those jerseys. You look like a sack of potatoes, not a dancer.''

She winced as she used the phrase. Calling them dancers. Recalling how, when she had trained, her teacher would say the same thing and how the magic of the vision would suffuse her as it caught at the wings of her and she was translated. Now she would do the same thing, just to see the image kiss these children and leave them marked, gloriously – but maimed for life.

She knelt and set about re-tying Pamela's ribbons. As she tied a firm and neat reef knot on the inside of Pamela's ankle, lumpy against such a small bone, she remembered she had not given Annabel her spare key although she was supposed to be spending the night with her.

She looked quickly over to the car park but, where the red car had been, there was an empty space. She looked back again at the children. Jane had shed her outer skin and left it piled on the seat of her chair. All the chairs were now neatly aligned, one behind the other.

Miss Pruett put down her paper and looked at her over her spectacles. ``Annabel gone?'' she asked.

`` 'Fraid so,'' Miss Streete replied.

``Poor kid.''

Miss Streete offered her a small wry smile. ``Grade three, if you're ready,'' she said.

``You haven't forgotten, I wanted to go five minutes early?'' Miss Pruett said, turning the pages of the music, looking for the piece she wanted.

``No, no, I hadn't,'' Miss Streete replied and then, watching her looking at the pages of music, said ``Oh let's not use the set music – let's have something more inspiring.''

Miss Pruett smiled at her, enjoying the compliment. She flexed her fingers.

Miss Streete turned back to the class, put her feet in first. ``Right girls, we'll have a *demi plié*, one and two,'' and she demonstrated: ``Rise, three and four, and a full *plié* five and six and seven and eight: in first, second and third. Ready? With the music now, arm to first, and a . . . no! Stop!''

Miss Pruett, surprised, looked round and stopped playing. She reached over and picked up her newspaper again, thereby distancing herself from the outburst.

Eight faces looked back at Miss Streete's, lathered white with concern.

``It's not good enough,'' she heard herself say. ``It's just not good enough! You are not ready. The minute you hear the music you must stand properly; be ready: every part of you, stretched, pulled up, ready to dance and, as that music starts and you lift your arm, the first movement you make must be saying `Look at me, look at this wonderful music, look at me: aren't I beautiful – watch!'

``Now let's start again; you must not just put your body through the movements; anyone can do that; you must think, use your brains.

``Feet in first,'' and she aligned her own feet as she spoke.

``Now pull up, knees tight, thighs tight, seat under, waist pulled up, ribs right away from your hips, now lift your chest, your chin, settle your shoulders down, stretch your neck, eyes up, head lifted, feel it: it is being pulled up on a string . . .'' and as she said each thing, she did what she was telling the children. ``Now with the music, lift the arm from your back and think – `I . . . am . . . wonderful!'

``Ready . . . and . . . ''

And Miss Pruett, right on time, picked up the cue and Lara felt again, for an instant, that mystical integration between her body and all the space in the universe meeting in a brief communion with her real self – then cast her eyes round her class. And of course it had worked. The sudden halt, the focusing of attention, her words, her body, had told them how, and now eight children stood, unfettered but enslaved, before her.

``Very good!'' she called out and then watched as they lost and regained control of their bodies. Recalling the instructions, pushing their muscles and stretching their tendons, making their bones ache.

``And on the other side,'' she said and marched to the end of the room.

``Well,'' she thought, after supper, ``if Annabel hasn't a key I'll have to wait up for her – if she decides to come here and not stay with the boyfriend.''

She took her plates to the kitchen and started washing up.

She remembered there had been six of them on the tube. She had been going to do a class and the other five were going to an audition.

Denise was pawing inside her bag. ``I've got to find those lucky earrings,'' she was saying. ``I haven't a chance if I don't find them."

``Oh God, do you think I should wear high heels?'' asked Rowena. ``They make my legs look longer and slimmer.''

``I'm not sure whether, if I get this, it'll leave me time to audition for the summer season at Scarborough,'' said Maxine.

``Come on,'' Rowena retorted, ``filming in the Greek islands or six weeks in blustery Scarborough – I know which I'd rather – and you'll probably earn in a day what you'd earn in a week there.''

``I think I left them at the hostel,'' said Denise. ``I honestly think I'm that dumb.''

``Come on now,'' said Bobbie, ``they are not looking at your ears.''

``Oh, that's not the point,'' said Denise petulantly, ``you know that's not the point.''

They drew into a station and Maxine glanced up at the name as it slid past the window.

``Should I have brought tap shoes?'' she said. ``I've forgotten if it said bring tap shoes.''

``I've got some,'' Lara volunteered. ``You can borrow mine.''

``We don't need tap shoes,'' said Bobbie. ``Honestly – it'll be stage and ballet . . . keep them,'' she said to Lara, who was rummaging in her bag for her white Oxfords. ``Put them away, Lara.''

``Perhaps I'll have them,'' said Denise. ``Just in case.''

``You could wear them on your ears,'' said Bobbie.

``Why don't you come, Lara?'' said Trudi, from her corner seat, where she sat, with her bag on her knee, almost hidden by a strap-hanging gentleman who overhung her.

``What's the point?'' said Lara, knowing her treacherous knee might betray her at any time. ``If I got it, my knee could force me to drop out.''

``But it might not,'' said Bobbie, ``It's bound not to be as rigorous as ballet and you're still fit.''

Suddenly, Lara was overwhelmed. She wanted desperately to play the part, even if she knew she was laying false claims to the status of a dancer. That and curiosity.

Glimpses of what might be whirled before her eyes. A large part of the activities of the stage school were alien to her. In many senses, she was not prepared for the world into which her ambitions and talent had precipitated her. She had come from a quiet, sober home, and the misgivings of her bank-clerk father and housewife mother. They knew nothing of the tumble and glitter, bustle and hysteria of this demi-world, the nursery and greenhouse for the theatre. In her first term, many of her classmates had landed themselves chorus parts in pantos; and their absence at the end of that, and the beginning of the next term, was completely acceptable to the establishment. Even that was a surprise; absence from her secondary school would not have been brooked, particularly if she had been away to be in a pantomime. She was shocked and thrilled at the same time. But classical ballet was her main subject, so she could afford to file all this activity away as something that need not involve her. And yet . . . and yet . . . even with a shattered knee, she knew that she cherished an unacceptable ambition. Before she had to give it all up, before this part of her life slid past her like one of the dimly lit underground stations even then sliding by on the other side of the grimy train windows, she wanted to be in a pantomime, or a summer show, or some revue; where she would wear the costume, the wig, paint her face, step onto the boards out into the lights, and move around in that exciting ritual called show business.

Now, as she swept the foam bubbles round the sink, she

wondered more sagely if it was better or worse never to have made that leap. For, if she had tasted that fruit, wouldn't the inevitability of her departure from her chosen career have been all the more difficult to bear – even more painful and desperate than it had been?

But that small challenge she had taken up on Trudi's suggestion excited and, indeed, flattered her, and she had followed the girls to the theatre, experiencing the same extraordinary ordeal that regularly humiliated Annabel. Perhaps she was emboldened by her armour of despair, knowing that she did not need the job and that her retirement from the stage had already been decided by external factors.

She had not been prepared for the hundreds of girls backstage, all changing into dancing gear, babbling and bubbling and surging. There was a lot of hair brushing, tights straightening, tucking away of straps, hitching-up of leotards, tying of headscarves, squealing and giggling and covert cigarette smoking going on. The unruly herd were rounded up and shepherded to the stage. A huge stage. The lights were white and saturated the air.

A young man in white T-shirt and jeans, holding a clipboard, ran to the wings; his frenetic energy seemed compounded of haste and self-importance. ``Right girls,'' he said. ``Singly please, centre stage, double pirouette.''

``Oh, good God,'' said Denise in her ear, ``I've not done one yet and not ended upon my back.''

``Do they mean a ballet one or a stage one?'' Bobbie muttered.

``Either, I should imagine,'' Lara replied, ``Oh look, there's Kay and Gretchen.''

``What *are* they wearing?''

``Dressed to kill is the expression,'' said Maxine, nastily. ``Sequins indeed!''

``Oh well, anything to catch the director's eye, I suppose,'' snarled Denise.

``Come on now, come on, let's get going,'' called the harassed young man.

A tall girl in a bright red leotard and bright red tight-fitting trousers marched boldly to the front of the stage, in the centre. She prepared for the pirouette, turned effortlessly three times, ended in open fourth, head lifted with triumph and bravura.

``Oh, good grief,'' said Maxine in Lara's ear.

``Thank you. Stage right, please,'' called a voice from the darkened well of the stalls. ``Next please.''

Lara watched, as girl after girl came forward and attempted the step. None managed the assurance nor the overwhelming redness of the first candidate. She watched with surprise at just how bad some of the girls were; at the outrageous and extraordinary clothes they were wearing, the amazing make-up. A couple of girls looked entirely classical: buns, black leotards, no make-up. The steady stream moved forward to centre front – the way they walked was in itself a performance; some strode, some sidled, some sleazed, some oozed, some paced, some prowled. They had five seconds, roughly, in which to ensnare the attention of the director, and some were determined to use every last millisecond.

Lara looked round, wondering where all the girls came from. They could not all be at stage school, she decided; some of them were just too bad, too unkempt and decidedly the wrong shape. Yet they all believed, each of them, in the little maybe, the outside chance-against-chance that they could be snatched up by the golden net and cast on the shore of stardom. They each had a dream, an ambition, an inner vision of a new and different world – and the courage, the bravado, the cheek, to step full across the ravine of apathy, trying to find the golden road to somewhere else.

She could see how ludicrous it might look to someone else, how inappropriate, unsuited as some of them were in terms of looks, grace and ability. She watched them, now diminishing them in her head, because they and she were adversaries. Two girls with towering beehives, vividly striped blue and white leotards and high-heeled silver shoes tottered forward. They tried the pirouette. They failed. They tottered to the wings. About one in thirty was asked to wait, stage right. Lara knew she could do a double pirouette perfectly well but, alone in the centre of a London stage, watched and scrutinised, – well, she wasn't so sure. And the longer she waited, the more nervous and unsure she became. `I'd better get this over, then,' she thought to herself.

Maxine and Denise were already ahead of her. Neither of them did very well. They passed her, looking ruefully at the wings.

Suddenly she was standing there.

Alone, in the glare of the lights. She tried to make out a face in the darkness in front of her, but couldn't. She started to prepare.

``Stage right,'' a voice called.

She walked to the small bunch of people, huddling by the flats, stage right.

She couldn't believe it – she hadn't even danced. What did that mean? Well it meant, initially, more of this ordeal.

In a flurry of giggles, Trudi joined her. ``My God, I'm through,'' she said. ``Well done, you!''

``Thanks,'' said Lara. ``Now what?''

``Denise and Maxine are going to change leotards and hairstyles and try again,'' she whispered. ``Look, there they are.''

Sure enough, Denise and Maxine were lining up again.

This time, the director told Denise to try the pirouette again, but still she couldn't stay properly centred.

``It doesn't help going into those blinding lights,'' Trudi said. ``I don't know how I got round; sheer fluke.''

Denise and Maxine sidled up to them, as a small girl with very classical features moved over to join them.

``Oh well, it was worth a try,'' Maxine said.

``Where are the rest?'' Lara asked.

``Bobbie and Rowena have gone; they don't want to miss Jem's modern class,'' said Denise, whilst Maxine turned to a lady who was pushing her way among the girls.

``You're not supposed to be here,'' the lady said, crossly and hoarsely. ``You were eliminated.''

``I know,'' she replied quickly. ``We're just going.''

``Well, you're cluttering up the place – '' push, push. ``It's not in order.''

``We'll wait for you in the café, over the road,'' said Denise. ``Good luck.''

The lady elbowed her and Maxine out of the way. ``Right,'' she said, ``you must read this,'' and she handed the waiting group pieces of paper.

Lara looked at hers. It was a job description. Eight weeks in Greece. Equity contracts. Wages Equity approved. Passports required. She felt overwhelmed, as though a wave was propelling her in a direction she had not anticipated. The film was called *Island Adventure* and would be starring a famous rock star and his backing group. She thought of Denise and Maxine, and how this job would be so much better for them than her and Bobbie and Rowena. She shrank. She felt a fraud – she had not even turned the required pirouette.

But now they were into the next stage of the journey. She wandered into the centre of the stage with the other thirty dancers and watched as a little young lady started putting together some steps, counting the beats and demonstrating the moves. She watched, she assimilated. From nowhere, a piano struck up some music. Then they were launched into the amalgamation. All of them, jumping and turning. They were divided into smaller groups. In fives they leapt across the stage.

``You in black, stage right,'' called a voice, ``you in pink, stage right. Thank you ladies.''

She ran stage right and the rest melted away, as in a dream. She watched. Trudi joined her, and more of the company dissolved in front of her eyes.

There were ten of them now. Ten from what – two hundred? Three hundred?

``How many do they want?'' she asked Trudi.

``Search me,'' said Trudi.

They watched the rest. The girl in red and the classical girl in dark were dancing now. They joined them. The red went. They were called back. The lady who had given the routine appeared again, and sheltering her eyes from the lights, she looked across at the stalls.

``Latin number, Nib?'' she called out.

``Either way, love, you decide,'' came the answer.

Another amalgamation. This time, fast frenetic and with the flavour of a rumba. Lara watched, perplexed. She moved through the steps, marking them, imprinting their shape and form, not so much into her head, but into the fabric of her muscles. The dance began as a cerebral process, but then became something less considered. Something intangible, woven into the web of her body. A statement she was making to the waiting world. Her own shape that she was making in space and time and, because she was making it, although the steps were not of her devising, a statement only she could make. She traced its outline with small movements of her

hands, her shoulders, her feet. Then she knew it, understood
it and wanted to make it.

The music started.

They all danced it.

They were subdivided. Trudi was in the first group. She
was not asked to stay. Five girls waited in the wings. Lara's
group stepped forward. As she launched into the *posé*, she felt
the familiar sickening pain in her knee. She stopped. She
moved backstage, and then turned to go to the dressing
rooms. It seemed an eternity since she had left her bag there
– and now it seemed remarkably deserted, smaller and less
occupied. She looked round at the few bags remaining and
noticed a teddy bear leaning out of one. She looked up and
saw her reflection in the mirrors, with their ring of naked light
bulbs.

`Well,' she thought, limping slightly and sitting down
heavily. `That is probably the closest you are ever going to
come to any of this.' She felt suddenly heavy, and looked up
to see Trudi standing by the door, her bag over her arm and
her mac. on, but still undone.

``You out, too?'' she asked.

Lara nodded.

``Oh well, good try.'' She paused and looked round. From
the distant stage came the sound of more music. Different
music. They had moved on into yet another routine.

``They're still at it then, up there?'' Lara asked.

``Yes. Do you know how many they want?''

``No?''

``Two.''

``Two?'' She could not believe her ears.

``Yup. The rest are cast already, evidently.''

``Two? From two hundred?''

``I think someone told me five hundred turned up.''

``You're joking.''

``No, that's the way it goes.''

Lara was quiet.

``You're ready?'' Trudi asked. ``Let's join the others.''

She balanced a plate carefully against a cup, surprised at how tense she had become as she relived this episode, how her heart was suddenly beating faster. She pulled out the plug. The water gurgled and ran away.

In the café, Denise and Maxine and Trudi had giggled and laughed, united in their effort, united in their failure. Lara had wondered how it would have been if one of them had got in – less convivial perhaps. And she wondered, too, how they would have felt if they were not still at college, but in the job market for real. Already she had seen tears in glittery eyes, the swallow and the slump of the shoulder blades in some of the girls who had not been asked to stay.

And to do it time after time; turn up, perform, and be rejected – what must that feel like, if not utterly demoralising?

As if in answer to her thoughts, Annabel pushed open the back door. She looked up at Lara and looked straight into her eyes. ``Thanks for waiting up,'' she said.

Later, when they were both sipping Earl Grey tea, Annabel tucked her feet under her on the sofa and said ``D'you know, I sometimes find it really hard to teach . . .''

Miss Streete waited; she knew Annabel wanted to say something else.

``And you must worry about it too,'' she added, a hint of accusation tingeing her voice.

``Why?''

``Because of selling the dream . . . it's like . . . '' she searched for an analogy and then found one suitably acerbic:

``it's like peddling drugs''.

Miss Streete was quiet and still.

``You know, all the time I was at ballet school they never once prepared us for the reality of the big wide world out there. It was, if they talked of the future at all, which was rare, it was always, when you are doing this or when you are doing that – never, if you are doing this, or, if you are doing that – with the emphasis on the mighty bigness of the word *if.''*

``I know what you mean.'' Miss Streete sighed and wrapped her hands round her cup and then breathed gently onto the surface of the tea, so that the aroma of it swept into her nostrils. ``I worry about that, as well. And the worst thing is it's not those that haven't got a chance. In a sense, they are going to be all right. With luck, they'll just remember dancing as a pleasant activity they did as a child and when they're grown up, perhaps they'll take their daughters along to dance classes too. No – it's the ones like you, Annabel, that keep me sleepless.''

And she smiled up at her – and Annabel, because she was good humoured, gave her an answering grin.

``What do you do?'' Lara asked, rhetorically. ``You see a shrimp with talent, the right physique, quick brain, right face, and the feel for it all – what do you do? Ignore them?''

She looked over at Annabel, who was flexing one of her legs, pulling it well past her ear in one of those unpremeditated and careless ways that dancers have of stretching and testing their limbs.

``What would you have felt if I had ignored you?''

``Very pissed off, probably.''

``Exactly.''

``And why?'' she added. ``Because you know you have the ability, the talent . . . the spirit . . . whatever it is . . . to experience the sheer joy of moving with the music, exactly the way you know you should – and I had the means of showing you how.''

``I know, I know,'' Annabel said, running her hand through her hair, pulling it back from her forehead, where it stayed, sticking up in the air.

``But all this job hunting, trying to get work, that's the real pain.''

``I know.'' Miss Streete gathered up the cups and moved to the kitchen, ``But then, either you join the board game and roll the dice, or you opt out, I suppose,'' wondering suddenly whether her injury, her compulsory retirement, was bitter or sweet, or if she had only exchanged one pain for another.

``I must go to bed, Annabel; will you excuse me?'' she said.

``Yes, OK; I'm off, too. I've an early start – I think I may as well try this one for *Tramps*.'' And she was seated, cross legged on the sofa, peering down over her legs at *The Stage*, spread out on the floor before her, perusing the jobs section.

``Oh, will you be back in time for the Grade Ones then?'' Miss Streete asked. ``They've got to get `The Sailor's Hornpipe' sorted out.''

``What time is that?''

``Five o'clock.''

``Oh yeah, Grade Ones,'' said Annabel, slightly abstractedly. Then, coming to attention, ``Which ones are they?''

``Oh, Rebecca and Rowan and . . .''

``Ah yes, Rowan; she's the little one with the fantastic turn out, isn't she?''

``Oh, you noticed her?''

``Mmm. She's very good; perhaps you should think of auditioning her for stage school.''

``Annabel!''

And Miss Streete watched helplessly, as Annabel laughed with her. ``You mention it,'' she suggested.

``Pass the opium pipe,'' Annabel replied. ``I'm off to bed.''

``Me too,'' and with that Miss Streete retired.

April Evening

AT the end of an April evening the dampness that had been
lying in the earth rose up as if with a yawn. The whole air
palpitated with vernal moisture. The smell wafted in through
the open windows, carrying with it a heart-rending fragrance
compounded of bruised lilac and lustful wallflower. She sat on
the sofa as one transfixed. The odour swept into the house,
pouring the garden smells into every dusty crevice, creaking
the old, shaped wood of furniture and mantelpiece till she
could almost hear it calling out for water. The flood of nature
exuded strange ideas. Half-remembered candles flickering
amongst spires of white-flowering honesty. It reminded her of
a time before she knew love but when she had first
anticipated what love might be. A romantic, wistful time;
fancy, frenzy and terror mixed in equal parts coupled with the
complacency of the slaughtered lamb. She knew she wouldn't
escape. She was right. She remembered now. Somehow the
mischief done by the spring flowers had unlatched hidden
doors. She saw his straight back, his cropped hair, his elegant
head perched nobly on his dinner-jacketed body. She
remembered that glimpse of him so well. It was one she
resorted to in dreams – when she was frightened she would
recall the cast of his face, the slant of his features. Because she
sat at one side of the crush bar in the Opera House and he
was at the other. And after she had noted him he had turned,
and with that way he had of lowering his head so that his

eyes appeared questioning beneath his eyebrows, he looked at her steadily and she felt herself shake slightly. And then the quick ravishing smile had stretched across his features – but more than that, his countenance appeared lit up as though he had a candle somewhere inside his skull. And she knew that he loved her. So simply. And that there was a future for both of them together.

She got up from the sofa and moved towards the french windows, wanting to pull them shut because although summer was supposed to be on its way it was still chilly. But she didn't; she opened them still further and stepped out onto the patio. The flowers opened themselves unashamedly to the night, their honey seeping onto the dew-fretted grass.

If she had known how closely they would draw together she might have had the sense to realise his parting would provide infinite grief. The temptation was to shut this spring out – to refuse to acknowledge that there would be other springs, when she had been shut so firmly in winter for so long. But that which had acknowledged all that youthful passion so many springs ago was still part of her nature now – and still beguiled her into the perfumed paradise lurking outside her living-room.

The slightest breeze ruffled the pink-dappled apple blossom. A few of the petals drifted to the grass beneath the tree; the mess of spring was already laying snow on the garden. She remembered the way he had bent forward to applaud at the end of *Fidelio*, the light from the stage catching his cheekbones and painting a Lautrec-orange smear on either side of his face. A curious mask of joy and severe features. Then she had leant against him in the taxi and there was an arm around her shoulders and another cupping the hand in her lap. She thought she would never be happier. And as she now considered it in retrospect she realised she had probably been right about that. Then all she wanted to do was to be a dancer and all he wanted to do was to be an airline pilot.

Over Dover sole and a very fine Chablis he had said ``Darling, will you marry me?''

And she had cast her eyes down, and in order to stop the rush of foolish sentimental tears had frowned at the unoffending fillet furiously. He took it for disapproval. ``I mean,'' he said quickly, ``once you have become a world-famous ballerina. May I throw flowers at your feet and escort you from the theatre to our little family home?''

If the train had not been late, if some other action had prevented the lorry being in the road where it was, if the tyre of his motor had burst, if the earth had slowed momentarily in its movement round the sun and held up time just for a fraction of a second, then perhaps the accident would not have happened, and all that promise, and that bright young life snuffed out. Pop! like that.

A rustling in the undergrowth caught her attention. Spoony, the next door neighbour's tabby was busying herself with some nefarious under-bush business.

Only occasionally would she feel again the giddy surge of aching love inside her. A phrase, a ripple of music, a poignant gesture would awaken it. Then she might step into an attitude, arch her neck, and slowly lift an arm into an open fifth. A few seconds earlier she might have said to her pupils `Listen to the music. It's your music, let it lift you through the movement.'

And she would surrender herself to the nearest galaxy and stretch out to the lonely stars.

Each time she would berate herself for self-indulgence but

on every occasion she forgave herself. What was there left to her? When he'd gone, she'd involuted, wrapping her dance classes like a carapace around her. Rarely did the hurt interior glance out beneath its protective layer. When it did, it was to recreate the fiercely strong tenderness that she had known only for a few months. Then her teachers would watch with the glow of the satisfied. Then she bestowed on her audience the searing scents of a spring evening. Seeing the look on her fellow students' faces, however, she was frightened. Frightened by the power she could unharness, nervous of the glances that mingled malice with admiration. She knew it was forceful enough to bring audiences to their feet. She knew she could stir every heart with a turn of the wrist if she wanted it. And yet – and yet – exercised alone this property seemed indelicate – inappropriate.

``Yes,'' she had said, and the bluebells glowed like ghosts in the unearthly light. ``Yes, I'll wait for you under the chandelier. And you can help me carry the bouquets home.''

His young face looked old and deadly serious. ``Our bouquets,'' he had said; ``you will be dancing for both of us.''

Without his sanction, somehow she had felt she couldn't.

She moved lightly down the path where the laburnum hung chandeliers of green racemes, pale jade jewels trembling slightly in the night air. She sniffed, and filled her lungs with the scent; freesias, forsythias, a sweet salt jasmine.

As he had said that, she remembered looking at his button hole. A white carnation with an asparagus fern winding spring green tendrils round the bluey green seaside stem. She remembered how her stomach seemed to fall out from her body, leaving the fish still in her mouth with nowhere to go.

As it was, she never had to make the decision; she knew the first time the knee gave out on her that her career had ended. As the days of rest were prescribed she watched the whole of what might have been borne away from her like leaves on a stream. Always things being carried away. Her white carnations amongst the wreaths on his pale oak coffin. But the love, the desire remaining – never really dying because it was the kind of love that could not turn away – even when the object of it was far far removed.

Like the greenness in the garden it came back, time and time again to swim through her. Swim with her. And sometimes she would let it lift her limbs and they would dance.

A Kind of Continuation

MISS Pruett put down her knitting (knit three, slip one) and extended her sensitive fingers to the keys of the piano.

``Ready – and – one and two and – '' came the voice. And the comforting chords of Chopin floated across the room.

She didn't need to watch. She knew what was happening. If she cared to glance up she would see umpteen little bodies in pink leotards, holding onto the rickety church hall chairs, pointing their toes to the front and to the side. The knuckles of the hands with which they held the chairs were white with effort, tongues protruded, little foreheads were shiny whilst tendrils of hair, straying from the pink headbands, were damp and clinging to the neck and temples.

In a far corner the sunlight slanted onto the floor and the dust motes, too, rose and sank in the melody-soaked atmosphere. A few mothers sat lumped on chairs around the edge of the hall. Each saw a vision of a ballerina, a delicate creature spun from glass, ethereal in her lightness, dreamlike in her spangled tutu, in place of the dumpling form of her own dear daughter. Eyes misted slightly, and heads listed gently to view better the promising curve of arms and legs.

``No, stop. Stop!'' came the command. ``Abigail, do you really call that pointing your toe?''

Miss Pruett's hands left the keys and searched for their knitting, the thumbs settling comfortably back into the soft warmth of the wool (was it knit three, slip one, or knit three and purl one?). She peered through her glasses at the pattern.

A shadow fell on the lower end of the keyboard. Someone approached. She raised her eyes. It was Jenny with her cup of coffee and a plateful of biscuits. She smiled and her hand reached out for the one with the jam in the centre. Immediate comfort. And why not? There was not much else that was very soothing. Not since she'd had the letter from the hospital summoning her to an audience with the consultant.

She sipped her coffee, and jumped suddenly to attention.

``*Grands battements*, Miss Pruett,'' came the command.

The hands, seemingly unbidden, found their own way through a Polonaise.

It was not that Miss Pruett was frightened of hospital – she wasn't. She had a proliferation of experience – her mother had for several years been in hospital; lying in bed making puppet-like arm and hand movements, her mouth agape, with Petrouschka's sad smile echoed in her eyes and eyebrows. And she herself had had her recalcitrant wrist restructured and resplinted in a hospital when she was only in her thirties. She knew when it was both sensible and appropriate to be brave. She struck an A major chord *con brio*.

The pupils threw their little legs into the air, tensing their tiny buttocks, drawing in their hips and screwing their arms into desperate curves.

``Stretch the arms,'' carolled Miss Streete, her lips tightening a fraction.

The door swung open and there stood Mrs Tureen with Elanor and Lucie in her wake. She blinked twice and a smile of determination settled onto her flaccid lips. Her girls had long since strained and stiffened their limbs at this elementary level. Indeed, she felt sorry for the girls who had stood by their chairs – called the *barre* by Miss Streete – on either side of her daughters. They could only feel diminished. Elanor tugged at her ribbons straggling down beside her ballet shoes, Lucie readjusted her brace. They watched their classmates struggling under Miss Streete's eagle gaze.

``Chairs away, girls. Come into the centre.''

Miss Pruett looked at her knitting – something was amiss – she gazed closer. Mrs Tureen moved into her customary chair. She felt the admiring gaze of the other pupils' mothers.

The pupils were swiftly organised into four lines by Miss Streete. Miss Pruett turned over several pages of music, Jenny wearily ran her gardener's finger down the crease in the centre of the register. She marked the presence of Elanor and Lucie. Annabel, Miss Streete's assistant, re-emerged from the ladies cloakroom where she had been admiring her new, flattering all-in-one. Miss Pruett shifted a little in her seat. Her grey weep-weary eyes sought the horizon beyond the piano, beyond the window, beyond the roofs of the dull suburban houses that sprawled between her and the southerly lying hills. No doubt she was being sensible. She gulped a little, took a sip of coffee and nibbled at a biscuit.

The pink forms kaleidoscoped across the room. Miss Pruett encapsulated their forms in elegant classical cadences, giving an import and significance to the movement that rested somewhat uneasily on the juvenile and stuttering forms. Miss Streete cajoled. The mothers sighed with contentment . . . Miss Pruett's music fuelled their wild and undisciplined dreams. Mrs Tureen urged Ellie and Lulu further forward into the limelight. By unobtrusively mirroring the pupils' actions they would practice their steps, demonstrate their knowledge and proclaim their prowess. It was rumoured that Miss Streete missed nothing. Mrs Tureen tweaked a frill into place and smiled an acknowledgement at Jenny. It wasn't as if she hadn't paid. Too true she had. Well, to be more precise

Stewart had. And why not? They were his kids weren't they? And if he wasn't going to perform all the rites and duties of fatherhood in the conventional sense – then he would have to pay the penalty for the unconventional sense. She certainly would not suffer the indignity of seeing that her girls were allowed to suffer. She was aware of a certain oblique set of her shoulders as she huddled back into her camel saddle-stitched coat. She crossed her legs and sniffed unobtrusively.

Miss Streete extended her gaze to encompass all. Her eyes glazed for the merest fraction of a second as they included Ellie and Lulu.

``Face *croisé*,'' she commanded, ``your exercise for attitude *à terre* in all directions.

There was a shuffling of feet; toes were turned out, hips waggled and eyes sidled furtively to their corners, surreptitiously watching what other girls were doing.

``Miss Pruett, please. Ready. And . . . ''

The knitting was left deserted again in her lap, the music soared. Her mind wandered. She had told Miss Streete about the op. as she might well have to miss a week's classes. Miss Streete was sympathetic but short, in her usual business-like fashion. Whatever was practical was best, was her simple philosophy. But Miss Pruett knew, because she was no fool, that certain tests had proved positive and the offending piece of flesh was going to be removed. She'd faced traumas before in her life, that was not the problem – but always they had been dealt to her by some external agency. She'd suffered jealous maulings from her sister since earliest school days. They seemed to grow more savage with age, not less, which belied the mellowing that was supposed to come with maturity.

She sighed. The music stopped. The exercise had finished.

``And now; a look at *arabesques*. Please try to keep your

back up, Cecilia, this time.''

The gentle twelve-eight rippled sympathetically across the room; the leotards wobbled and faltered. She could hear Miss Streete tutting. Ellie and Lulu, however, launched into flawless arabesques; chins lifted like avenging angels, legs braced, toes and fingers straining away from each other.

Mrs Tureen's head drew back a fraction. Certainly her girls could dance. Stewart's defection could no more deprive the girls of their talent than it could deprive the birds of their song or the earth of its natural rhythm, although she had found herself surprised and even affronted when the crocuses opened their gold and purple petals and the hazels hung up their jaunty catkins, announcing the spring that had followed that awful, awful winter. She couldn't believe how sore were the parts of her that were damaged after he had torn away from her. The wreckage seemed so fundamental she couldn't believe in the new forms coalescing in the gardens and woods around her. But the onus of regularity of attendance at the girls' different classes imposed a rhythm and order and finally a shape on her, which convinced her of a kind of continuation.

``Now consider this *enchaînement*,'' called Miss Streete, ``*glissade devant, jeté devant . . .* ''

The voice faded as Miss Pruett mentally assessed rhythm and tempo. She shuddered. How could her own flesh have turned traitor and dealt her this blow? Unless it was self-inflicted. The very sinister implication of this idea appalled her. She couldn't believe in this brutality; the type we might call down on our own heads. She knitted four furiously and slipped one and knitted four again.

``But Samantha, *devant* means in front, and Kirstie that *pas de chat* must have the knees turned out – No! facing the walls! and for heaven's sake point the second toe. Well, let's try with the music.''

Shoulders lifted and then lowered, tummies flattened and the little fingers twitched.

Despair settled on a dispirited trio in the back row. This was where their feet knitted and knotted into each other – never to be untangled. Miss Pruett dropped her knitting, a jaunty six-eight cajoled life into the earnestly pointing feet. Ellie and Lulu scampered backwards and forwards on the side lines, performing the steps to their and their mother's satisfaction. Miss Streete's eyes skidded past them as she scanned the flying legs for misplaced third positions – she swiftly excluded the back-line trio. She knew when and where to conserve energy.

Miss Pruett noted the splodge of sunlight on the floor had moved. It crept nearer Mrs Tureen's chair. She knew a bit about Mrs Tureen. Jenny had received and fielded some harsh confidences and a few had filtered through with the coffee and the biscuits to her end of the studio. She looked at Ellie and Lulu – and understood immediately how they knitted their mother into the warp and weft of the week. The flesh round Mrs Tureen's tired eyes sank floorwards with earth-seeking insistence. Suddenly the eyes moved from a steady consideration of the dancers to Miss Pruett's own. They smiled. They smiled with undisguised affection. Miss Pruett's head swung heavily away under this alarming assault.

``Girls, please,'' called Miss Streete. ``Let's try it again, and remembering all the things I've said. Abigail, those are not dead fish at the end of your legs – they are feet – point them.''

The children sniggered at this unexpected levity at Abigail's expense. And the *gigue* music was reconstituted by Miss Pruett.

``Better, better,'' called their teacher, ``much better. You can use your feet so well when you try, Abigail. Now *changements*

. . . who can show me . . . ?''

Mrs Tureen watched Ellie and Lulu springing in the air like young lambs. Indulgence flooded her. Miss Pruett might have escaped the rigours that her own separation had brought, but she hadn't the satisfaction of seeing her children, swollen with talent, unfold like rosebuds. Then Mrs Tureen hesitated slightly. Was it worth it? The music for the jumping steps rolled around the room. Life had to go on, she supposed.

Miss Pruett glowed with a gentle camaraderie. She contemplated Mrs Tureen, who also had suffered an amputation. Parts of her had been physically removed. She wouldn't be the same again. But she lived – she moved through a pattern of activity that was her life; even though it was centred on a couple of talentless, lumpy children who were generally considered less than pleasant. For as such had Miss Streete in a moment of confidence described them. But Mrs Tureen had pulled through.

``Thank you girls.''

Miss Pruett sought the knitting pattern again.

``And the curtsey – no Ellie and Lulu, this is not your class; please wait.''

Ellie and Lulu, unaffected by the gentle admonishment, joined in anyway. Miss Streete's smile moved momentarily in and out of a sharp-lipped rictus. As they said: she missed nothing.

The curtsey music flooded through the relieved and exhausted dancers. It suffused the contented bones of the watching mothers.

Miss Pruett caught Mrs Tureen's eye. She returned the smile. After all, they had a lot in common.

The Conjuror

WHEN I saw the curtains: I knew the magic was mine. Now I can be the conjuror, I can create the dreams and trances that swim from that magic box. I never asked Daddy why he did it – spent an afternoon in the summer's warmth fiddling with the old blackout curtains on the washing line, plying backwards and forwards with pieces of rope, fumbling with string and curtain rings, a cigarette hanging from his mouth, puzzling and blundering and then calling us all to see – when lo! he stood at one end, by the post and pulling on the ropes, he made the curtains divide. The wall of black severed the lawn, on one side the little flat area where the crazy paving path wanders into a flower bed and on the other the gentle slope that rises and pours away into the upper lawn. And there it was – my own magic domain. Now I had the power in my palm.

Celia and I plundered the toy cupboard and dragged out a box for our scrutiny. We unpacked the spangled stuff, the crumpled cotton, rumpled net, the swathes of drapery, old shoes, frilly hats, bonnets with long blonde plaits tied to the corners. There were twinkling sequins, little green crêpe paper leaves, the rich indigo wealth of a velvet ribbon and the trappings of a thousand *personae* all waiting to be given life.

I wondered again at their incredible beauty: the zig-zag indentations at the end of a net skirt, the silk roses and paper flowers; the parasol, frilly gloves and long elegant mittens, pink satin bows, the cardboard crown smothered in gold paper with silver-encased ping-pong balls adorning every spire, a cupid's bow and a cap with cat's ears, a paper lantern, a furry hat and the wand of the fairy godmother.

I lifted a green chiffon scarf and let it fall again, softly, softly to earth. Its mist became the light of a moon maiden's flesh. In a cloud-burst I smelt again the grease-paint: plasticky and smoky; felt again the lurch and tumble of excitement, the white milky coldness of fear in my stomach, the sweat in my armpits, the goose bumps on my flesh. Standing in the wings I trembled and all the silver edging to my tutu shook with me – I heard Mrs Bonner strike the notes of my music. `Go on now, it's your music,' the voice whispered and I stood waiting whilst the lights dazzled and burnt and the chords rippled away, climbing into their place waiting for my moves – and how I rose and lifted my arms and swung forwards and down and through into the moves of the dance – the pause from the audience – the glare and focus of attention on me – and then through me and then out – out from my arms and legs and body into the great trembling space of the stage.

And then the wait, the smile of relief and the run-off of tension to the relaxation of the applause, my curtsy, an acknowledgement and the overwhelming desire to do it all again, but better this time and then again and again – re-calling that rapt attention. Watch me! Watch me! Watch! Then into the next measure as the other dancers walk slowly round, remembering places and moves and shapes and positions. And all of us wheeling and re-convening and concentrating as it goes according to plan.

And coming off and watching with baited breath the big girls – the ones that look like real ballerinas, gliding through steps so complicated that it makes me weep with joy and envy and amazement. Stretching their legs so high into the air, moving with arcane wisdom into patterns beyond my comprehension. Thrilling me with the promise of what will be mine to master in times to come.

Then scuttling along the dark corridors behind the stage into the dressing-room – stripping off my dress and looking on the rails for the next one – and a big lady coming up and dropping something over my head and pulling me in front of a mirror where large red patches of red make-up are put on my cheeks and big black lashes spiked out from my eyes, a bonnet put on my head and an apron tied over my blue dress – because now I am a china doll – and lined up with five other china dolls – all shrilling and twittering in the darkness of the dusty way to the stage, where we're put in order – and the grey straight figure of our teacher, papers in one hand, beckons over our heads to some unseen person in the background.

The light swamps and blinds as the curtains part and I go through the mechanical moves of the dance – I am hard, brittle and parts of my body do not move. Click and clack – I jerk and stutter – this is the clockwork, harsh and unrelenting, pushing my spasmodic movements. Suddenly I see Janet has gone the wrong way and is in danger of being missing from the circle we should make. She is lost in the maze of the dance and we have to rescue her. I push out an arm and hiss and she realises her mistake – the pianist plays some extra bars whilst she adjusts and the circle re-assembles. Now we are ready for the next part and all seems well. But now Ann stumbles and I look up, seeing the frantic movements from the curtains that shroud the wings. Our teacher is gesticulating, twisting a finger in the air: we have forgotten the turn on our toes – I see her, comprehend and imitate her movements – the other dolls realise their mistake too and, seeing what I do, copy and carry on – but Janet has ignore the cue and wanders, unhinged, into some other part of the stage. I sigh and take up my partner and we skip round and round – hoping no one has noticed – knowing that we have made the great mistake – we have gone unutterably wrong – we have broken the rules and deviated from the steps of the dance. Covered with shame, we scuttle to the safety of the wings, whilst the lights on the stage dim. I look back to the darkened scene of our shame – shrouded and hunched now, small and mean. Oh to have another chance – but it has gone – gone. The audience are clapping – but we are undeserving – we lost our way and are derisory now. We are hustled, cheeks aflame, down the narrow creaking steps that lead back through the echoing corridors to the cold sanity of the dressing-room and to the fierce accusatory lights of the day. I look for the teacher – waiting to see her frown of disapproval – but all I get is a smile and then notice her sudden switch of attention – because now a large group of the little ones clutching paper nosegays are being mustered under her anxious gaze. She has forgotten, as swiftly as the curtain fell and the lights dimmed on the performance; the mistakes and the glory both have gone – extinguished like the moth in the flame of the candle.

Now I have a hoop of paper flowers in my hand and to the rousing chords on the piano we make loops and arches and weave complex patterns with each other. After the line the circle, and after the circle the arch. We weave and glow and flow and smile like summer flowers and because all the intricacies come right and the dance ends with the last chords on the piano as we skip round the stage and off, the audience smiles too and claps and the sound of the applause drowns the notes of the piano. Hooray – I think – hooray – at last we did it right – we defeated the mistakes and the blunders and we brought something – and I briefly wonder what – to fruition. And then as I see my teacher's face I know; it was her dreams that had shifted, slid from her to us, become shape and form and real, and she had made this magic.

Now I will make mine.

Celia, I say, we must use this and that and Francesca. And we look with doubt at our baby sister. So we swathe her in veils. Surprisingly, she is uncomplaining. She smiles and dimples and we explain carefully what we want. Her dimples paint pink apple blossom into her creamy skin. She is sunny and acquiescent and so I love her. Celia finds the cupid's bow and tells her to hold it; I am busy winding up the gramophone, putting the needle carefully in place on the record when Daddy pulls the ropes to open the curtains, and with a hiss, and a splattering, the thread of music pushes through the waterfall of crackles and sings out a thin and tinny melody. I climb into one of the white frilly dresses and glance at our audience. Granny and Grandad and Mummy and Aunty Tabs are sitting in deck-chairs on the slope, smiling at Francesca running up and down by the path, waving her arms and twirling on her toes. The hissing announces the music is over and I fold back the arm of the gramophone, then rescue Francesca, who is bemused by the applause, and drag her to me. Celia steps forward solemnly, pink-faced and frowning with concentration, and starts saying her poem. It is called `Little Trotty Wagtail' and lasts long enough for me to turn the record over and wind up the gramophone again. The audience laugh and clap at Celia's poem and Daddy pulls the curtain closed. And now it's open again and the music sings tinnily for me. First it's cold white fear I feel, and then the sudden hot flush of embarrassment; this is hard – a sudden dichotomy – I'm not supposed to show off, I've been told so often. But now I must – because how else can I show them? For them to see the dance and like it properly I must show

them all they need to see and at the same time pretend the
mistakes and the inadequacies aren't there. I have to make the
pretence. I must balance and control the toes, the head, the
arms; I have to prevent them falling away, flying away from
me, pushing apart into the sky, tumbling into chaos – they
must move whilst the music compels them and these shapes,
this writing, has to say what I want it to mean.

Then when the curtains close finally I am compounded of
excitement and exhaustion, rolled into a heavy and yet
quickened whole. Our audience have applauded their last.
Francesca sits on Mummy's lap and sucks her thumb; Celia
and Granny are giving Grandad and Aunty Tabs cakes and
lemonade. Daddy, with an eye to the sky and the threatening
shower, is swiftly dismantling the curtains and sheeting.

Suddenly I am confused. Was I what they wanted me to be?
Indeed they did smile, they did clap and their applause
seemed to be approval. Was I what they expected – or not?
Why else had those curtains been hung there – except that the
conjure man in me should have been drawn forth, wheedled
out, eviscerated (like the guts from the Christmas turkey).
Now another curtain seems to have fallen between me and
them. Their reticence and strange apartness is like a mist
between us.

Have I disappointed them? Was it me or was it my
performance that disappointed, distanced? Are we different
things? Which of them do they love – and from which now
like a tide have they withdrawn, leaving me dry and bone-like
on the shore? Which me? All of me feels bereft. There is a
dimming of light, just like the gathering nimbus in the sky. It
engulfs my crouching, confused and increasingly hesitant
body. There was the white brightness of the performance, but
now a dreadful darkness encroaches.

The green smell of approaching rain rolls from the tree tops down across the garden. The magic has suddenly gone, swept away by this capricious, inconsequential breeze. The sense of loss and over-crowding dark curdles my heart. Something heavy and grief-laden weighs in my chest. Perfunctorily I put the black gramophone discs back into their blue paper sleeves in the album. Turning the pages and their previous burden carefully, my sad eye falls on a maroon label – and I read the gold letters. I remember the tune, it sings in my head, and suddenly I think – we'll use this, we'll use this next time. And the drag of disappointment flies away – only this will hold the dark at bay. Yes, Yes my heart sings, the next time – of course there will be a next time – and I anticipate rebirth, deliberately defying those dark clouds.

Taking New Steps

NOW the new term was beginning. There was already an autumnal nip in the air. The sun fought with wreaths of mist to clear his face in the mornings, and the spiders were hurrying inside the houses for shelter or spinning dense matted cobwebs in the hedgerows. The leaves had lost their fresh green lustre and looked old and tired on the trees.

Jenny was sitting at the table gathering up the fees for the forthcoming term, Lara Streete was talking to Clara Pruett by the piano and Annabel was stretching her legs at the front of the hall, with a cup of coffee in her hand. Jenny looked anxiously over at Miss Streete; she was soon going to need assistance with the little crowd of new parents that was beginning to crowd round the table. Lara caught her glance and extricated herself from the details of Miss Pruett's walking holiday in Scotland.

She walked smiling up to the table, glancing at the clock as she did so.

``We'll start as close to half past as we can,'' she said to Annabel as she passed her; ``I expect we'll get later and later during the course of the morning, anyway.''

She came over to the parents.

Jenny said quickly ``Here's Miss Streete, you'd better have a word with her.'' With her eyes, she indicated a young mother, clustered about with her two daughters.

Lara started talking to them. She established the girls'

names and ages, found out that this was their first dancing class ever, ran an eye over them for their suitability of dress and persuaded the mother to take off their shoes and socks.

Annabel had started assembling a circle of the babies, as they were rather demeaningly termed, chatting to the ones she knew about their summer holidays.

Lara took the two new girls by the hand and led them into the circle. The younger one turned round, anxiously looking for her mother, and made to pull away from her.

``Mummy's watching,'' she said; ``don't worry, she won't go away.''

The girl looked at her suspiciously.

``I'm going to stay with you, anyway.''

Her big sister was already giving her attention to the circle they were joining and was striving to hold the hand of another little girl, who was locked in serious conversation about her forthcoming birthday party with Annabel.

``Hold Beth's hand,'' Miss Streete said to her, and she stopped chatting and did so.

Annabel said ``Sarah's having her birthday party today.''

``Gosh, that's going to be exciting isn't it?'' Miss Streete enthused.

The small girl at her side chipped in. ``It's mine next week.''

``Is it, Siobhan?'' Miss Streete answered, ``and how old will you be?''

``Four,'' the girl replied.

``Four!'' Lara exclaimed. ``That's pretty old isn't it?'' and the little girl nodded enthusiastically. She looked round at her sister and, seeing that she had joined hands in the circle, started to do the same.

Annabel launched into the lesson and, as Miss Pruett started playing the piano, the circle of children watched her and struggled to imitate her actions, turning hands at the same time as their feet in an effort to get the actions right.

Once they got to skipping round the hall and Beth and Siobhan had forgotten their shyness, Lara judiciously retired. She walked over to the mother, who was now sitting on a chair with the other watching parents, clasping the children's coats and shoes on her lap.

``They'll be OK,'' she said, and then sat down herself by Jenny, watching the newcomers. Swiftly she summed up their potential, although hardly conscious that she was doing so. She noted their build, their bone structure, the length of their Achilles tendons, the flexibility of their feet, the height of their arches, their musicality, their ability to keep in time, their own absorption in what they were doing. Beth she had already noted as serious, diligent but of a slightly heavy build, Siobhan on the other hand was lighter, more slender and lyrical. Annabel asked them to do little runs round the hall and to wave their arms at their sides as they were doing it.

``Make your arms very, very light,'' she said; ``they are floating at your side,'' and she showed them what she wanted.

Miss Pruett started up the music. Miss Streete watched. Siobhan had caught the feeling exactly, and was light on her feet as well. Furthermore, she had a way of holding her head that slightly mirrored and emphasised the movements her arms were making. Lara nudged Jenny and indicated Siobhan.

``Good, is she?'' said Jenny.

``Well, look at the way she's moving her head,'' Lara replied.

Jenny watched, but inwardly thought that at least three other children were moving with as much grace.

``Mmm,'' she said.

``Did we get all the names and addresses of the new parents?'' Lara asked.

``Yes, I think so,'' said Jenny. ``A couple rang up before term began and gave me the details then.''

``Oh good. Have we got many new ones?''

``Umm. Only about as many as have left,'' Jenny said.

``Oh dear,'' Miss Streete sighed, ``I was hoping numbers would pick up again this term. I really wanted to be able to pay Annabel more. And really I think Miss Pruett is due for a rise. All we need is for Mr Conway to shove up the hall prices and I'll be losing . . . again.''

Jenny refused to be daunted. ``Some more may come along during the course of the morning,'' she said, ``and we do go on gathering up new ones right up to half term, don't we?''

``We'll see,'' said Lara darkly. She turned her attention from the register, which she had been scrutinising, back to the class. Annabel had the children sitting on the floor, clasping their ankles, with their legs spreadeagled so that their knees were nearly touching the floor. They were bouncing their knees up and down in time to the music. Annabel had perfect turn out and her knees rested quite comfortably on the floor. Lara looked round the circle of children. Quite a few were managing to do the same thing and she noticed with satisfaction that one of them was the newcomer, Siobhan.

Now the children had stumbled to their feet and Annabel was trying spring *pointes*. The children who had mastered this step last term were doing well, but the newcomers were finding it difficult, the temptation to put the weight in the wrong place being the most common pitfall. Annabel went round to each of them in turn and as Clara Pruett accompanied them they each had an attempt at getting it right. Annabel held their hands, trying to push the weight back onto the supporting leg and doing it with them at the same time. Beth and Siobhan bobbed up and down hopefully with the rest of them but still hadn't mastered it when it was time to do some more jumps, this time travelling round the room.

``It's that dreadful fear of letting yourself down in front of other people,'' Miss Streete said, speaking half to herself and half to Jenny. ``I remember it so well – ''

Then to her dismay she noticed that Siobhan had left the group of children and had run up to her mother, tears in her eyes.

``What's the matter?'' her mother enquired.

Siobhan wouldn't say, and consequently her mother didn't know.

But Lara knew; and she guessed correctly that Siobhan would certainly not say anything to her mother if her mother hadn't already noticed.

Determined that the little girl would not go home with a sense of failure still in her mind, Lara stood up and came over to her. ``You've done so very well for your first lesson, Siobhan,'' she said, ``it would be a pity not to say thank you to Annabel for teaching you, wouldn't it?''

The child was silent, looking on at the class, immobile and serious.

``Do you know how we say thank you in ballet?'' she asked.

``Thank you,'' said Siobhan quite promptly.

``Oh no,'' Lara laughed, ``you have to remember that dancers don't speak. No. We do a curtsey. That's a step. It's quite hard as well; you have to be careful not to fall over. And the boys do a bow.''

At this point, most opportunely, Harry stepped forward to give his bow to Annabel.

``Thank you Harry,'' Annabel said. ``Now girls, your curtsey.''

``Let's go and try, shall we?'' said Lara to Siobhan.

And Siobhan, consumed with curiosity, was already leading Lara forward into the centre of the hall with the other children so she could try this new step.

Miss Pruett played the music very slowly, knowing that this was new for some of them, and knowing that Annabel would want to talk them through it.

She did.

``Leg behind, Siobhan,'' she called, ``not in front; that's it; and bend both knees together. Carefully. Well done. That's it, Beth. Right, and now on the other side. Step to the side and put the other foot behind, bend the knee, Joanne, right; on the toe, on the toe, try and keep a gap between your legs; you remember the window we had when we were doing the bends? Good. Right and bend. Hold your dress, carefully. Good. Well done. Thank you.''

And Miss Streete looked down at Siobhan's shining face. ``Well, that was excellent, a beautiful curtsey. Well done Beth,'' she said as the older sister came up. They looked at her expectantly.

``You can go to Mummy now.'' And the two girls scampered up to their mother, who looked extremely tired as though she had performed every step with the children herself.

Already another pool of parents was issuing into the hall as the departing class pushed out through the doors.

Miss Streete looked up at Annabel, who was perusing the dance syllabus book.

``You doing this one as well?'' she asked.

``Yes,'' said Annabel; ``anyway, I need to remind myself of it, especially a couple of the set *enchaînements*.''

``OK.'' She came back to the table and said to Jenny ``I'll take over the register if you want to get another cup of coffee going.''

``Good idea,'' said Jenny and, taking the teabags and coffee cups from the cupboard, pushed through the sea of parents into the kitchen. The side counters were piled with children's clothes while the floor was strewn with ballet shoes, socks, hair brushes and ballet cases. She put the kettle on and slowly the children gathered up their outdoor clothes, stowed away their leotards and cross-overs and drifted out of the kitchen, leaving Jenny to contemplate the steaming kettle.

For Jenny another term was beginning as well. At last, at long last, she had persuaded her father to move into sheltered accommodation; and now she would be able to sell the large Victorian villa that the family had occupied for the best part of a century and get herself somewhere reasonably comfortable that she would be able to manage on her own. For years now the housework had been getting too much for her, and coming home from work and facing the chores had become a nightmare. And as her father became increasingly more frail, trying to keep him happy and comfortable on top of everything else, even with a visiting home help, was more than she had energy for. Had it not been for being able to get out to the dancing classes she sometimes thought she would go mad.

She wondered where her new-found courage had come from but dated it from her summer holiday when an act of folly had somehow resulted in a new surge of confidence. Holidays were usually a visit to her aunt's with her father, but when she died last spring that was no longer a possibility. After Christmas Miss Streete had asked her what she would be doing that year and Jenny had confessed that it was likely to be the back garden.

``What with an invalid father and the dog to look after I honestly don't think I shall manage to get away at all,'' she had said.

``I think it's because of the dog and your father you ought to get away,'' said Lara rather primly. ``Even if it's only for a week or ten days.''

Jenny pulled a face.

``Look,'' said Lara, ``if you don't mind me being bossy I'm going to suggest that you do. I'll look after them both if necessary.''

This spurred Jenny into action and she arranged for Jarvis to go into kennels and made extensive enquiries from the Social Services and managed to ensure that a home help and a nurse would visit her father daily.

When she told Lara all this, Lara countered by saying that she had been talking to Annabel and she was quite happy to have Jarvis for some of the time and she would do the rest.

``Anyway,'' she said sensibly, ``you don't want outrageous kennel fees on top of the expense of the holiday. And he knows us both so he won't fret. And if your father is getting proper medical attention then I shall just pop in every day to see how he is getting on and chat to him. It's not as though he can't get up some of the time and I'll be someone he knows he can talk to.''

``Do you honestly mind?'' Jenny asked.

``If I did I wouldn't have offered,'' said Lara, ``and nor would Annabel. Now all you have to do is to book it up and go away and enjoy yourself. That's an order.''

And they both laughed because she was being so bossy.

And Jenny had. She had found a small villa party that was going to Turkey and included in the price was a sight-seeing journey inland. So she could add a little touring to sunbathing; it seemed an ideal combination.

She was pleasantly surprised to find that all the people with her were independent, hard working folk like herself and had no difficulty at all lying on the sand one day with some of them, visiting the shops or restaurants or nightclubs with others. So the group who piled into the minibus for the tour were already familiar to her and she trundled off into the sun-baked interior with a sense of great adventure.

Two days out from base, after many a dusty mile had been measured by the bus, she contracted the most fearful sore throat. A visit to some nearby caves had been arranged and although she had managed to get some antibiotics she felt exhausted and faint. Inland Turkey sweltered under temperatures that approached the hundreds in degrees fahrenheit; even the rocks seemed to be melting under the fierce onslaught of the sun. She cursed the inopportuneness of the arrival of the disease and bemoaned her fate under a fig tree while the rest of her companions disappeared into the crannies in the shimmering amber limestone. Suddenly she knew that she had to get back to their overnight hotel and lie down. Emboldened by pain, she sought out the courier who arranged for her to be quickly returned to her bedroom, where she lay slightly delirious, drifting mercifully into an odd dream-ridden sleep, while the hours slid away into the hot breath of the day. By night she felt better and was able to gather with the rest of the group in the courtyard of the hotel as the waiters slopped up in their slippers, serving tea in glasses from silver trays and the courier, who was a closet scholar, read poetry to them as the stars wheeled up into the navy sky.

Perhaps she was still light-headed from the aftermath of the onslaught of the drugs, or perhaps she had a prescience of her ability to become autonomous, but suddenly she felt light-hearted.

The following night they arrived at the coast whence they were to turn their noses westward and wend their way back to their resort.

The night fell suddenly, the hotel was of an indifferent standard, there was no air conditioning and no fans provided. She felt for the first time the strange stickiness that settles on the skin that is the result of high humidity.

The party ate on a balcony overlooking the sea and as they did so a large ship sailed into the adjacent port, sounding its siren. This was the last night of the expedition and the wine flowed freely. Jenny was usually circumspect and invariably limited a glass of wine in the evenings to the weekends, and then when she was having her dinner. This evening, however, the dusk settled round her with hot sticky fingers and she found she was drinking to assuage a thirst that never entirely disappeared.

A group of four of them, all ladies, decided to take a walk around the town before turning in for the night. Although Jenny felt tired sleep seemed very far distant.

``What on earth is there to do in this one-horse town?'' grumbled Minka, while Jenny laughed at the expression.

``We'll walk to the quay and back,'' suggested Jean; ``find out where that ship came from.''

They did, slightly inebriated, cracking jokes as they went.

They enquired at the dockside, of the driver of one of the cars that were obviously waiting their turn to embark.

``It's going to Cyprus,'' was the reply.

``I'd like to go to Cyprus,'' said Minka. ``Who's coming with me?'' She looked round at the group, daring them.

``I will,'' Jenny found herself saying. ``I'm game if you are.''

``Right,'' said Minka; ``let's find out when it goes and what we need.''

So they did. It transpired they needed passports, and their fares and the ship sailed at midnight. They had half an hour.

Maureen looked crestfallen.

``I've left my passport back at the resort,'' she complained, ``otherwise I'd come with you.''

``You're mad,'' said Jean. ``What'll you say to the courier?''

``Oh, tell him we've jumped ship and we'll make our own way along the coast,'' replied the intrepid Minka. ``Come on,'' she said to Jenny; ``we've got half an hour. Let's go back to the hotel and get together an overnight bag. I'll leave a note to Bob. He's sensible, he'll make sure our other luggage gets on the minibus.''

In a dream Jenny put together the things she needed, the very barest necessities. All the time her heart was pounding in her chest. She had a wildness in her head and she could hear herself saying to herself, `you mustn't chicken out now.'

They reported back to the quay, where Maureen and Jean stood waiting. Three more members of their party had gathered to watch their act of folly.

They left their bags at their feet and rushed over the road to purchase their tickets from the shipping line office, then joined the queue to have their passports stamped. The watching group turned and waved at them as they moved towards the boat and were swallowed by the maw of the vast uplifted bow. Jenny followed Minka as they climbed up the companionways to the topmost deck. There they were greeted by the crew as though they were royalty and given seats in a little enclave that appeared to be for officers only. They were proffered tea and water. Luckily the sailors' English was not good enough to catch the rapid whispered exchanges that Minka threw at Jenny.

``I'm assuring them that our husbands have just waved us goodbye,'' she said, as she smilingly turned down an offer to visit the chief electrician's cabin.

The siren sounded, the Turkish flag was hoisted and the

stars swung in gentle arcs as the boat swung itself away from the harbour mouth.

The invitations to spend the night with various members of the crew grew apace. Minka fielded them laughingly while Jenny, slowly becoming sober, started wondering what she was doing on a car ferry in the middle of the Mediterranean sailing to Cyprus and who knew what.

The other passengers in the boat, from whom they were so obviously separate, started settling down for the night voyage. The boat was scheduled to arrive at seven in the morning. Most of the passengers were peasants, who seemed to be travelling complete with all their household effects, all of which looked like large sacks of potatoes. Even their wives seemed like large sacks of potatoes. They lit little fires and started spreading out food, distributing it and eating it. The *badinage* with the crew continued, as different members tried their luck with these odd eccentric English women who had so unexpectedly landed in their midst. As various of them realised that their luck was very definitely not in that night they drifted away. Minka was quite adamant in her explanation that their husbands would not like it. The night drew on, the engines purred and Jenny, several cups of coffee and glasses of water later, realised that with sobriety came a dreadful fear. But she couldn't go back. Even if she wanted to, here she was and she would have to see it through. The boat plied its way gently through the waves. The night air was balmy and still warm. Eventually the spirit of gallantry arose and Minka muttered to her that they had been offered a cabin for the night.

``Without escort?'' Jenny enquired.

``Without companion,'' Minka confirmed.

``For both of us?''

``Yes,'' said Minka, ``together. Shall we go and see it?''

They suffered themselves to be escorted down the steps
and into the interior of the ship, followed by the curious and
wondering glances of the sacks of potatoes. A chivalrous sailor
had proffered his cabin for the night. Tiny and twin-berthed,
but most welcome. They had to admire the photos of his vast
and extended family and talk to him at length about the
glories of Earls Court where his cousin was now residing, but
eventually he retired and bid them goodnight. Minka jumped
up and tested the lock: a practical woman. She settled herself
on the top bunk and immediately fell asleep, the sound of her
snoring blending gently with the background throbbing of the
ship's engines. Jenny was to enjoy no such peace. She nagged
at herself for her irresponsibility, she fretted about her father,
her dog. She dreaded what Cyprus might be like. She had no
terms of reference. Her jauntiness, her daring, her bravery had
all gone. Now all she knew was overwhelming fear.

The night drew on . . . and as is inevitable, morning came.

Jenny and Minka watched the approach of Cyprus from
the side of the boat, grey misty peaks already delivering up
their moisture to the heat of the sun.

They docked. Jenny gathered together her night bag,
relieved that she had been brutal when packing it and that it
was so light. She herself felt quite giddy with lack of sleep
and stepped onto the sunwashed stone jetty, feeling distant
and removed.

The scene at the customs shed was beyond belief.
Suddenly all the sullen, solid bags of potatoes had become
animated and there was a tremendous surging and thrusting
into the building. Minka and she walked towards the black
seething mass.

Then Minka turned away. ``I'm not prepared to be part of
that scrummage,'' she announced with disdain. ``Let's wait
until it has eased up a bit.''

She sat on a nearby wall and smoked a cigarette, her fair insolent face turned skywards. Jenny sank down on the ground then, unperturbed, put her head on her overnight bag, stretched out and hallucinated: it wasn't a sleep, it was a series of wild and vivid visions swirling in front of her eyes.

``Is your friend dead?'' enquired an arriving passenger to Minka, on seeing Jenny.

``No, she's sleeping,'' Minka replied coldly.

`Ah but,' thought Jenny, `something brave died in me last night.'

After a while they resumed their fight in the customs hall, where matters if anything had got worse and not better, possibly because by this time many of the invading Turks were getting very irate. Minka conjectured that the Cypriots were so terrified that all and sundry were invading terrorists or illegal immigrants they had a policy of keeping everyone at bay. Eventually she decided she was having no more of it. With Jenny in her wake, she gathered up a policeman and announcing loudly that she was British and that she would advise every one of her friends against visiting Cyprus until they got their immigration policy sorted out, she barged through the black-clad, dark-browed peasants like a knife through butter. Several of the more astute Europeans, similarly impeded, followed in her wake and they ended up outside the shed, their passports stamped, with two Swedes and two Danes in tow.

Minka hailed a taxi.

``Do we know where we're going?'' asked Jenny.

``The shipping office,'' said Minka. ``We had better check that these are return tickets and they'll probably know of somewhere we can stay.''

And that is how they found the Kangaru Taverna in Kyrenia. Jenny flopped on the bed, trembling and shaking, trying not to notice the blood stains on the white washed walls, where passing previous occupants had taken desperate swipes at the mosquitoes.

``You eat a packet of crisps,'' said Minka sternly, producing some from her bag, ``and get a bit of shut eye. I'll size up the joint.''

``I'm not sure I could manage any crisps,'' Jenny gasped.

``You'd better, it's for the salt,'' Minka said, all-knowing; ``that's why you've gone all shaky; you sweat the salt out of your system when it's as hot as this. I know,'' she said, with allusion to her more colourful, more travelled past.

Jenny lay back on the bed. She looked at the naked light bulb as Minka disappeared into the shower room.

``This is pretty disgusting,'' she called cheerfully from within.

``Oh really,'' groaned Jenny, ``what have you found?''

``Nothing actually,'' Minka called. ``It'll do.''

Jenny dozed. When she awoke Minka had returned, having had a full blown breakfast on the sea front. She sat on the edge of the bed and relit a cigarette.

``I think a little sight seeing, a little shopping, supper down by the harbour which is quite delightful, a night here and then the boat back tomorrow morning,'' she mooted. ``Do you agree?''

Jenny nodded.

So that is what they did, all the time Jenny feeding herself crisps and feeling herself gradually ceasing to tremble. Minka fitted herself out with Benetton sweatshirts and exotic perfumes. Evening at the waterside of the harbour was tranquil and delightful. They were plied with more dishes than they had room for, and due to a slight uneasiness with the language found that the food they were eating was considered as appetisers, which were free. Two very large brandies also seemed to come free with the coffee.

``Can't grumble, really,'' said Minka, ``even if we had rather got the wrong end of the stick.''

When they returned to the ramshackle Kangaru they discovered a piece of discarded bread from Minka's picnic for the homeward journey was covered with ants. With a cry Minka seized it and ran to the balcony where she hurled it into the night. There was a dreadful cry and a desperate clattering of bins. She gave Jenny a guilty grin.

The following morning, well provided with provisions, they sauntered off in search of a taxi and arrived at the quay, now bathed in peace and sunshine, the barbaric scenes of yesterday's seething crowd quite forgotten. Jenny presumed they had all got through eventually, although a part of her would not have been surprised to see them all still there, shouting and jostling.

Minka chose a part of the boat that would provide a useful suntrap and Jenny went in search of some deck-chairs. She found two and they arranged themselves along the bulkhead with towels draped over the tops of their chairs like the tents of the Bedouin.

The boat sailed, and from their peaceful secluded part of the deck Jenny and Minka sunbathed and read. Minka lit a cigarette and Jenny tried a crossword. When it was time for lunch Minka opened a large bottle of *rosé* wine and started disembowelling a large honeydew melon. They drank each other's health, only to notice on the deck above them a line of tanned faces. They were providing the in-cruise entertainment for a consignment of Turkish soldiers, obviously going home on leave. Nothing deterred, they carried on with their lunch, munching olives and cheese with the salvaged remains of the bread.

The sea was so calm that the ship made no movement;

there was just its gentle forging forward to the mainland.

Some of their acquaintances of the previous night came and conversed in their broken English.

``Our husbands are looking forward to our return,'' announced Minka loudly and emphatically. The young men nodded their heads and smiled their white-toothed smiles. The soldiers, sated with the on-going cabaret of their picnic, wandered away. Jenny did a little sunbathing and sipped at the wine. Minka slept. Jenny was overwhelmed by her friend's *sang-froid* and desperately envious of her coolness of demeanour.

`Why can't I be like that?' she asked herself. `All that self-assurance; why, I almost cripple myself with my self-doubts and my fears. I prefer the worse because I haven't the courage to find out about the better, let alone take steps in that direction.'

It was nearly dusk as they arrived back at Tususcu, steaming in on the night tide, just as the ship had done the night before last. It had been a long time since they were in that one-horse town, as Minka had put it so derisively.

Now there was no excited, disbelieving little band on the quayside to witness their adventure. They set off to find out about the buses and the whereabouts of the bus station. Despite the rapidly oncoming night the heat was stifling. Jenny felt the perspiration dripping down the inside of her shirt, trickling down her chest and settling round her waist. She looked down at her skirt. It was black and she noticed a white tide mark, well below the waist band. She remembered that the same mark had been there earlier in the day. But higher. She considered. And then remembered what Minka had said about the salt. This gently descending line must be sweated-out salt, left as a deposit on her skirt. No wonder she had needed the crisps.

Eventually they found the bus station and sat there as darkness fell, while all around the men played dominoes, the children fought and squawked and the dogs sat and scratched themselves.

Suddenly two sailors from the ship walked up to them and offered to buy them a glass of tea. They couldn't refuse. Then the bus arrived and the young men, chivalrous to the last, carried their baggage and saw them onto the bus.

They had seats right behind the driver as they started racing along the coast, pursuing their party which had already taken the same route.

Every time Jenny came out of a strange hypnotic dream, which she could hardly call sleeping, she sat watching the numbers on the signposts diminish twenty kilometres by twenty kilometres. Minka beside her had put her head on her shoulder and drifted into a heavy sleep. Every now and again they stopped and travellers would alight and new ones get on. After a stop the driver came round with lemon water and sprinkled it into each pair of proffered hands. And people would wipe it gratefully and wearily around the back of their necks, across their brows and along the back of their hands.

Finally the bus arrived at the end of the road leading to their resort, leaving about three miles to go. They had disembarked with two Dutch girls with whom they agreed to share a taxi. They walked straight past their villa and down to the water front, and there they watched the sun rise up out of the sea. The sand was quiet and strangely deserted.

Jenny felt an extraordinary peace spread over her tiredness. But something else as well, a strength and an unwonted sense of pride.

She and Minka were assimilated back into the villa party and a few days later she was back in England. The holiday over, the adventure done. But it had left its mark. On arrival home she set in motion all the necessary events for her father's care and her own independence. She was taking new steps.

Miss Streete came out into the kitchen. She glanced at the kettle which had boiled and turned itself off. ``I just thought I'd give you a hand,'' she said, and started putting a couple of tea bags in the pot. ``I think that little Siobhan's going to be good,'' she carried on, chatting to the teapot, ``but she was having trouble with the spring *pointes* – I know they are quite difficult.''

``She'll get the hang of them,'' Jenny said. ``After all it was very new for her this morning.''

``Yes,'' concurred Miss Streete. `` 'Course she'll get them. She only has to keep trying, after all.''

Jenny nodded. She knew.

The Lord Giveth

``NOW,'' she said, ``come into the centre. Let's look at the *port de bras.*''

The early autumn sunshine oozed through the misty window panes. Miss Pruett readjusted her spectacles and turned over a couple of pages of music. She looked up expectantly.

Amidst the scraping of chair legs, the children moved cautiously into the middle of the hall.

``Front row; Jane, Sally, Sarah and Vicky.''

And four girls, warmly wrapped against inflooding winter, eased their way forwards. More names were called. Slowly the serried ranks spread themselves out and over the floor. They turned their pink faces towards Miss Streete.

She pushed her feet in their pale pink Greek sandals into a fifth position and lifted her chest and then her arms. ``En croisé, come on Melanie – you can turn your toes out a little more if you try a little harder. First *port de bras*, girls. Ready . . . and . . . ''

Rippling arpeggios in a sedate twelve-eight plucked visions from the air. A dozen fairy-like ballerinas, gossamer skirts swirling round their legs, swarmed out of the immature bodies and described prescribed arcs in space.

Miss Streete ran her eye over them all, a glance swift and light as a butterfly's wing. She enveloped them all, noting the strained necks and heaving shoulders.

93

``Remember: relax, relax,'' she called. ``Enjoy it, you are unutterably beautiful! Melanie, relax those shoulders.''

Melanie's stiff arms propelled themselves around her body. Miss Streete sighed inwardly.

Miss Pruett progressed through a series of rippling sevenths and her hands spread themselves comfortably on the tonic. The sunlight faded abruptly as the clouds rolled in from the west.

Miss Streete wondered how soon and how quickly she would be able to get away at the end of the class. How easily she would make the connections on the long train journey that would carry her south and through the mellowing countryside to her – oh so recently – bereaved father.

The class continued.

Melanie's mother was standing between her and the autumn day when she finally came back to the table, where Jenny sat huddled over the register, the coffee cups, and the tin in which was collected the money.

``Might I have a word, Miss Streete?''

Availability was one of the additional services on offer. Miss Streete laced up her smile. ``Of course, Mrs Chapple; what can I do for you?''

Melanie's heavy form disappeared momentarily through the door as she made her way to the cloakroom.

Mrs Chapple took up a stance that meant business. She wanted a confirmation of her daughter's talent. She confided her plans for her gifted offspring. Miss Streete engaged her attention by attempting to look interested and sufficiently impressed.

``So you see, Miss Streete, with Melanie's grandparents so eager to help our children, and what with Robert off to boarding-school in September – we really wanted Melanie to audition for the Hurst Academy.''

Miss Streete knew that it was the major ambition of most of her pupils to audition for their nearest nationally-recognised ballet school. Mentally she ran her eyes over the mental image of Melanie: attractive, musical and responsive and considerably hard-working. She gauged her musicality, her quickness of response, her desire to please. She considered her innate danceability. In short, she auditioned her in a couple of seconds. Then she considered her build and compared it with her mother's. They were both built for comfort and not for speed, as the expression goes.

Mrs Chapple chuntered on, her soft compelling voice wrapping Miss Streete's instincts in clouds of persuasion. She stood in her crimson coat, matching stockings, and shoes by Raine, in a beam of light that as soon as it irradiated her was extinguished.

Miss Streete glanced quickly at the clock. Time was getting on. Miss Pruett was packing away her music. Jenny had rushed away to the kitchen, taking a tray with the dirty crockery. The hall was emptying.

Miss Streete had already made up her mind. She knew all her children were well taught – children who had not got into the Hurst Academy had not failed because of poor training. Her classes, although they were run in a modest way, in a modest building, were of the highest order. Melanie would get in. She had the right kind of background. The parents were sufficiently middle classed and well heeled and arts conscious enough for their progeny to pass muster. She nodded.

Mrs Chapple's eyes lit up. ``We can go ahead then?'' she asked.

``I should ask for a prospectus first, and visit the school,'' Miss Streete advised, ``and then if you are still happy, we will put in for an audition. You know, she will have to play a musical instrument, more than one if she can, sing and say a poem.''

``Oh, she's making exceptional progress, I am told, on both piano and violin,'' interposed the mother, ``and her teacher says she sings like an angel.''

``Well, that all helps,'' said Miss Streete crisply.

Mrs Chapple's daughter put her arm eagerly through that of her mother.

``Come on Melanie,'' said Mrs Chapple, ``we have to collect Daddy and have a chat.''

Melanie looked Miss Streete full in the face.

``Miss Streete wants you to try for the Hurst Academy,'' her mother continued, ``isn't that exciting?''

Melanie's eyes shone and she nodded.

Miss Streete, wondering on how many other occasions her name had been taken in vain, gazed back at her with a fondness that belied her thoughts.

Mother and daughter, all smiles, beat a retreat.

``That one trying, is she?'' said Miss Pruett, coming over with her shoulder bag in place and her music under one arm.

``Seems so,'' Miss Streete sighed.

``Mother seems to have got it all sorted out.''

``What's new?'' Miss Streete agreed. ``She'll be the size of an elephant by the time she's fifteen,'' she added quickly.

``Very likely.''

Miss Streete closed the register and gave Miss Pruett her envelope.

``Are you going to catch your train?''

``Not unless I ride like the wind.''

``Do give my condolences to your father, dear,'' she said.

``I will.''

``Will you stay long?''

``Depends on how he feels, I think. Anyway, I have to be back by Tuesday. Annabel can't stand in for me.''

``Can't she?''

``Seems not.''

``Where was she today?''

``A christening, I think.''

``You are too kind by half to that girl.''

Miss Streete kept her own counsel. She turned to the cupboard and stowed away the music and books. She looked round the room. Jenny came in again and they stowed away the cups and saucers.

``I'll say goodbye then,'' Miss Pruett said.

``Bye, and thanks a lot,'' said Miss Streete.

``Bye,'' added Jenny.

Miss Pruett sailed out into the wind-strewn day.

``Can I give you a lift or anything?'' Jenny asked.

Miss Streete was picking up a neglected cross-over and a forgotten pair of leg-warmers.

``No, don't worry, Jenny. I'll leave my car at the station. It'll be safe enough, and I need it there when I come back.''

``Drive carefully,'' said Jenny softly, ``and give my love to your dad.''

``I will.''

Miss Streete abandoned herself to the train journey. Occasionally visions of her mother soared across the saffron landscape and then she would turn her face to the window, whilst a great lump arose in her throat. Only once, on the outskirts of Basingstoke, did her cheeks cool to the insistent sliding of silent tears. She caught sight of her face reflected in the window, a travelling mirage, whose down-turned mouth disturbed the horizontal line of fences and hedges.

Her father was waiting for her when she arrived at the house. She fell into his arms as the taxi turned round in the narrow driveway between the brutally trimmed cupressus hedge. They sobbed quietly together.

Then as they both held cups of tea he told her how it had all happened. How quickly her mother's life had been taken away. How suddenly all that presence had gone. How strange and empty and void the world now seemed.

Miss Streete could not encompass the shock. She walked quietly in the garden amongst the quietly dropping plums, staring at the bubbles of grey fungi that speckled the skins of the well-rotted fruit. She could hear her father tapping the saucepans together as he made himself busy in the kitchen. She couldn't believe that she wouldn't look up and see her mother standing at the kitchen door – calling her, asking if she wanted another slice of cake, peas and beans with her supper or whether she had noticed how well the michaelmas daisies were doing this year.

She felt sobs surge through her body.

She looked up at the silver-rimmed, plum-purple clouds.

``I just don't understand why,'' she said to herself. ``I am totally uncomprehending. Why Mummy? Why?''

She retraced her steps, and saw the stooped shoulders of her father, bent over the vegetable rack, selecting some potatoes. Firmly, and running over with compassion, she insisted on making the supper.

They looked at each other. They caught the fearfulness in each other's expression. Silently they exchanged acknowledgement of each other's mortality. Her shoulders heaved, as her father's face crunched up with grief.

That night she heard the breeze savaging the leaves in the trees. She took refuge from reality by making plans for the future. She re-ran the interview with Mrs Chapple. The vision of another child assailed her. This was dark-eyed Paula, a child in the same class as Melanie, very possibly the same age. Paula was solemn and stately and serious. Her dancing was not ready yet for show. It was inward conversation. It was a dialogue between Paula's body and Paula's soul.

Miss Streete had one acid test for her pupils. She would ask Miss Pruett to play any music and she would urge her pupils to dance anything. Occasionally she put a story line into their heads. At other times she would let the music tell the story and ask the children, once they had heard it, to dance the story. It was improvisation. Then the real dancers emerged. To Miss Streete those with talent stood out so keenly that it was as though already they occupied the centre stage and the limelight of a follow spot was already on them.

Paula was one of these.

She was, as they say, a natural.

If anyone should audition for the Hurst Academy from the class it should be Paula.

She heard her father's footsteps pacing the well-worn route from bedroom to bathroom. She remembered her mother's side of their bed, the spectacle case and slippers and the books she had read. She heard the steps of her father who had a nail of him torn away from him. She was aghast at the swiftness of it all – one moment her mother's voice on the phone sounding free and optimistic, the next moment she was bound in the irrevocable iron hoops of death and her closest family flung into appalling grief. She cast her mind swiftly over her parents' contemporaries, companions in old age, even now planning the parties they would enjoy for their golden-wedding anniversaries. Why had her mother been denied the normal life span allotted to man? Why, she might have seen her married at last and a longed-for grandchild placed on her grand maternal lap. If there was a destiny shaping our ends, why was it so ill-conceived? She tossed and turned as the November gales reached the silently screaming skeletons of the trees.

The train journey offered a kind of solace, the hopeless joy of being in neither one place nor another. Suspension between places gave the illusion of suspending time. The carriage lurched and jerked as she cast a jaundiced eye over a landscape scarred with the detritus of ill-kempt industry. In the country the tractors dripped blood into puddles and in the car-yards of the towns the oil spilled rainbow tears across the pools of new-fallen rains.

Hurtling from one environment to another, she re-orientated her thoughts, her compass.

Four days later the grade-two examinees were mustering for another lesson. Miss Pruett was unable to be present so Miss Streete had to count her class's way through the exercises.

``And a one and a two, and a three, point your toes,'' she sang, not in rhythm. ``Stretch those necks, drop the shoulders and tuck in those seats.''

Melanie and Paula were one behind the other. Together they lifted their arms, from *bras bas*, through first to second. Together they pulled up waists and chests, and their heads lifted like heavy flowers to a proud and noble stance. Miss Streete watched. To give Melanie her due, she was working her little heart out. But Paula, Paula glowed with that special magic quality – it was suddenly saying `look at me – just look at me.' Miss Streete had seen it before, but it was its rarity that made her heart beat faster. Experienced as she was, she could not disobey that injunction. The child, the person who dances like that is simply obeyed. As the class progressed she found it increasingly more and more difficult to tear her eyes from the little girl.

Slowly the girls who were to take part in the next class started seeping through the door into the hall.

``Thank you girls; and your reverence, if you please.''

Faces hot with exertion looked up at the reprieve, and

relief flooded their concentrated features. Ten third positions were prepared and the *chassés* performed as the children thanked Miss Streete for her half hour of criticism and cajoling.

``You have worked very hard,'' she added. ``Well done. Paula, is your mother collecting you?''

Paula shook her head.

``She's working. I have to go straight to my child minder.''

``Will she collect you on Saturday?''

``She doesn't usually.''

``Could you tell her I would like a word with her? Perhaps she could ring me sometime?''

``Yes, I'll tell her,'' and the solemn faced child looked up at her. There was a dark intense look in her eyes; a hundred gypsies massed by a fire, hypnotised by the pagan ritual of flame.

Miss Streete glanced at the next class. Some were already practising *pliés* at the *barre*, others were stretched out on the floor, teasing flexibility out of taut hamstrings, chatting to their friends. A couple more were watching her talk to Paula. They knew.

The funeral was to take place on Thursday. She arranged for Annabel to take the stage and tap classes and the Friday classes. Sometimes it was not easy. Annabel had a complicated home life and it affected her work. If she was very depressed or very elated she became very serious about her dancing and was an admirable teacher. If, however, she felt half-hearted either about her home life or life in general, then dancing slipped like every other activity into a kind of sub-world where it had no importance in her life whatsoever. Nor did anything else. Miss Streete was not always able to predict whereabouts Annabel was in her cyclic life. One couldn't always tell by outward signs. A new leotard and matching leg-warmers would not necessarily denote a renewed enthusiasm for the Art, new vows taken as a devotee of Terpsichore.

To belie her mood the sun had made one of its pungent, late-in-the-year appearances. The beech trees flared torch-lights of burnished leaves, the golden groves were unleaving, the sky a flood of cerulean blue. A sleepy drunken tortoiseshell butterfly stumbled from golden rod to the lilac-fretted michaelmas daisy, then took its velvet robes to the crimson eye of a sunburst dahlia. The coffin handles glinted coldly in the sunlight that surged through the church window. The sun seemed to shout resurrection whilst in her ears beat the antiphon: death, death is the end of it all. Two such opposites cannot possibly go hand in hand. You cannot mate such strange bedfellows. The paradox screamed sorrow over the dusty funeral flowers.

The babel of relatives eating their way stolidly through ham sandwiches and fruit cake built up a curious conviction that her mother's memory was larger than life. The shadow her death had cast conjured a legend, strangely embellished, that made her slightly unrecognisable. Conceding her many and varied qualities, Miss Streete felt her mother's reality slipping further and further away from her, passing as a dream does when one wakes dismally to the cold light of morning.

That night as she lay in the same small corner bed that had been her own when she was a child she thought `I can't get from life what I want. And now I can't get whatever my mother had to give me, and I can't get what I want for my pupils.'

And she rolled over in desperation at the dreadful futility of it all.

That Saturday Paula's mother came to see her. A little later than expected, so that the class was already well into their *ronds de jambe*. Paula had changed in the cloakroom and was sitting quietly watching, her legs swinging back and forth, tapping against her pink ballet case in which she had her shoes.

As soon as Miss Streete saw her mother she moved towards her, and called Annabel to take over the class. She caught Miss Pruett's eyes, lifted slightly above her spectacles as she watched her move up the hall.

Paula's mother was pale and nervous. Her hands were gnarled and a garish lipstick imparted a desperate glamour to her heavy-eyed face. ``It's no good, Miss Streete,'' she said. ``I'm on my own, you know. Paula lives for her dancing, but it's as much as I can do to send her here, particularly if she has an extra class now and again.''

Miss Streete glanced at Paula who was watching the tremulous *attitudes en l'air* with a droll solemnity. Out in the car park she saw the silver cigar shape of the Chapples' Volvo slide out of its parking place, bearing Melanie back to the family residence.

She sighed. ``But you know,'' she rejoined, ``the local authority would help; they would assist you if they thought Paula was talented. And I have every reason to believe that they would.''

The affirmative chords of *temps lié* rang out, and the bodies swooped and dived as arms soared and flowed. Miss Pruett teased the tangled chords, spreading their petals. Annabel posed on one pink *pointe* shoe, admiring the satin, admiring her flawless arched foot, admiring her firm thin young leaping legs, just admiring. Jenny rattled in the cupboard, searching for the teapot.

A couple of mothers sat, shoulders inclined to each other,

exchanging luscious tit-bits of news, revelling over the interchange, ignoring their gasping daughters.

She saw Paula's mother sigh – sigh with the heavy desperation of one who, already battle scarred, fears the next fight.

A fight it would be, too. There was no guarantee nowadays that a talented child would be helped financially. Even if the school accepted her the local authority, too, would have to make a decision: too many talented children applying in one year and cuts would be made. Quite discriminately. Miss Streete had heard and seen it all before.

She watched Paula's mother.

Annabel started the first steps of an allegro *enchaînement*.

``A mazurka will do nicely, Miss Pruett,'' she called in her treble-flute.

Paula was on her feet marking the steps, face rapt.

``I'll think about it, Miss Streete,'' the mother managed, but she was already defeated.

``I'll help all I can. You know that,'' Miss Streete said desperately.

The woman tried to smile.

``I could give Paula three lessons for the price of two?'' she continued.

``What do you mean?''

``Well, Paula could stay and do this class as well – look, she is doing pretty well already – and it can only make her better.''

The poor woman looked nervous and suspicious by turns. One of her hands pulled at a coat button.

``Right,'' called Annabel. ``You've had enough time to mark it – off we go. Ready . . . and . . .''

The mazurka carved its Polish cadences into the white wood surface of the cupboards at the back of the hall.

Paula and her mother departed.

``There's a little one with promise,'' revealed Miss Pruett. ``Money problems, I suppose.''

``You've guessed,'' conceded Miss Streete.

She fingered the pale turquoise ring her mother had worn as a `dress ring', as she had in her quaint old-fashioned way called it. She gulped as she drove home through the rain, the bright puddles scattered like pools of mercury along the roadside. Amidst the welter of water she allowed the tears to fall.

The autumn fruits were scattered at random along the de-leaved hedgerows. Here a blush of scarlet hawthorns, there a sprinkling of sloes. She mentally reminded herself to give her father a ring and wondered whether she could snatch another break to see him. She could picture him now pottering in his greenhouse, tending the pampered vine which was already quite heavy with grapes. Ah well! The Lord giveth and the Lord taketh away. She thought of Melanie and Paula. To some He might appear to take away before giving. She abstracted herself quickly from the overwhelmingly incomprehensible injustice of life.

The shower stopped. From the north a cold wintry wind started to blow.

Le Baiser de la Fée

THE small figure was standing beside the door of the main dressing-room. There was a kerfuffle along the corridor that led to the wings of the tiny theatre. Three toadstools and a pond complete with cardboard weeds was being manhandled off the stage. Cupid with his bow and arrows was rearranging his wings that were threatening to get even more lopsided. Two nymphs were standing red-faced and panting alongside her, trying to help. The arrows tumbled out of her quiver and fell to the floor. The mythological creatures fell to their knees and in the semi-darkness tried to locate the bamboo sticks with their oven-foil ends. One backed into a toadstool and it fell in two pieces across the cardboard pool.

Miss Streete looked at the scene.

``Let's clear these props,'' she whispered, ``they're in everybody's way here. Hannah, Penny, give me a hand.''

``We're on any minute,'' whispered one of the nymphs.

``Oh, go and get ready then; don't for heaven's sake miss your cue.''

The nymphs and Cupid stood up, hastily reassembling the quiver, and giving a last tug at the recalcitrant wings.

``I'll do this.'' The goddess Artemis appeared from the darkness and with silver fillet complete with a crescent moon tipping forward over her brow she helped Miss Streete drag the toadstools and pond towards the dressing-room.

The elegant figure stooped as they shambled past.

106

``How's it going, Lara?'' she asked, a smile hovering on her lips and a twinkle in her grey eyes.

Miss Streete looked up at the voice, her face streaked with two grey stripes of dust. ``Alice!'' she cried, and an expression of delight washed over her fraught features. ``I expect this is slightly familiar?'' she then asked.

``Oh, just slightly,'' the other replied, and held the door open while they negotiated the props into the dressing-room where they were stowed under a table swimming in make up and cotton wool.

``Thanks, Tina,'' Miss Streete said to Artemis, who smiled briefly and then fled back into the wings for her next entrance. ``You managed to get here,'' she went on.

``Well, yes; only because Richard drove me.''

``He's here as well?'' Lara asked.

``Yes, watching the show with the children.''

``Oh great,'' Lara said. ``What a devoted camp follower.''

``Well, you can meet him later.''

``Have you seen any of it?''

``Yes,'' Alice replied. ``Lovely! Wonderful costumes!''

``Well, that's Jenny,'' Lara conceded. ``You've met her, haven't you?''

``She's the one who came to mine last July, isn't she?'' Alice asked.

``Yes, that's right,'' Lara said. ``Sit down. It's nearly the interval.''

``No. I'll get out of your way. You'll have things to do.''

``No I won't,'' said Lara confidently. ``They all know what they are doing. It's surprising really; once it gets under way, I find myself surprisingly redundant.''

``Really?'' said Alice. ``I find myself in the wings, every moment chewing my fingernails and agonising.''

``Yes,'' countered Lara, ``but there's not much point is

there? There's not much you can do if they do all go wrong."

``Except have kittens," said Alice, laughing.

``And backstage is awfully smooth. I have a band of wonderful mothers who keep an eye on the kids, keep them quiet and occupied. If I flap around I'm accused of interfering. Which I probably am." She laughed. ``So I have to act cool, calm and collected as though nothing matters."

``That's hard enough," Alice agreed.

Lara, hearing the strains of music seeping through the door, said ``Yes, that's the end coming up now. As long as the stage crew are paying attention and remember to pull the curtains, all is well." And even as she listened she had a picture of what should be happening on the stage.

``So when's your next one?" she asked.

Alice sighed. ``Never," she replied. And they both laughed because this was the stock answer.

``Why don't you repeat *Cinderella*?" Lara asked. ``That was one of your best."

``You say that because you were in it," Alice replied. ``Ugly sister doubling as some kind of fairy, if I recall."

``Ah," said Lara, ``my first *tutu*. Do you remember how my mother laboured over it? And how proud she was when she had finally made it?"

``She was a good mum," said Alice, ``even though you were always quarrelling with her. How is your father, incidentally?"

``Oh, he's managing marvellously," Lara replied.

Two girls came in and started stripping off their clothes. They were talking quietly to each other, and one looked for the other's shoes whilst the other picked up their two head-dresses.

``I shall go," said Alice.

Liam's mother came in with his costume over her arm.

``Lara,'' she said, ``have we any stain remover?''

``What for?'' Lara asked.

``I'll see you after the show,'' said Alice. ``Richard will be looking for me; he'll wonder where I've got to. I'll wait in the front bar.'' She smiled and added ``good luck for the next bit.''

Lara smiled. ``Later then,'' she said, and turned back to Liam's mum. ``You'll never guess who that was,'' she said.

``I'll guess she's a dancer,'' Sibyl said immediately.

``How do you know?'' Lara asked.

``Oh, it stands out a mile,'' Sibyl continued, ``the way she holds herself, feet turned out . . . you know, there's always something about dancers that makes them look . . . like . . . well . . . dancers.''

She smiled. Jenny came into the dressing-room with a small boy whose braces had snapped. She started looking for a needle and cotton.

Annabel called from in front of the mirror. ``How is Jane to have her hair?'' she asked.

``Pony tail,'' Lara answered.

``Was that Alice I saw?'' asked Jenny.

``Yes,'' said Lara, smiling. ``I'm so glad she's managed to get here. She is loyal.''

``And then the head-dress goes round it,'' Jenny was explaining to Annabel as she threaded a piece of cotton through a needle.

``She was my teacher,'' said Lara, full of proprietorial pride.

``Oh,'' said Sibyl. ``Jenny, have you anything to remove this stain?''

She showed Jenny Liam's costume with a big red stain by the upper sleeve.

``What on earth has he been doing?'' asked Jenny. ``He's been kissing the girls again,'' she laughed.

``He wouldn't have a red stain here, now would he?'' Sibyl laughed.

``Kathy gives him a kiss on the forehead, anyway,'' said Lara.

``Aah,'' said Sibyl. ``I bet that's what's happening, as soon as he comes off stage he wipes it with his sleeve.'' She tutted. ``Silly boy. What can we do?''

``I've got something in my bag,'' called Annabel, ``that might do the trick. – Is this right?'' and she held Jane's head by the pony tail and turned it round to show Lara.

Jenny looked at it critically. ``Half a mo','' she said. ``Let me finish this and I'll come and give it a tweak.''

She hastily finished sewing the braces and pushed the child away from her. ``There you are, John, that'll have to do. Don't twang them so; that's why they snap.''

The child ran away and she turned her attention to Jane. Annabel dived into a basket under one of the tables and handed a tube of something to Sibyl, who started rubbing away at Liam's collar.

``Have you seen my wand?'' Kathy asked and started rummaging through the debris on the table.

``You'll never find it like that,'' said Lara and started searching with her.

``I left it here, I'm sure,'' said the Snow Queen, her eyes panicking under her glittering eye make-up. ``Oh no! I didn't. I put it on that table in the wings.''   ·

``Oh heavens!'' said Lara. ``I hope for your sake it's still there.''

Kathy ran out.

Sibyl held up the sleeve. ``Better?'' she asked. ``I know it's not perfect. It'll have to do.''

Lara looked at her watch. Five more minutes of the interval. She dashed down to the other dressing-room and looked in on a group of children clad in red and white, some snow flakes and some snowmen. They were sitting on each other's laps and the bigger ones were reading to the little ones. Two mothers stood chatting to each other while one was plaiting the hair of a little girl who stood in front of her. Several snowflakes were lying on their tummies on the floor colouring in pictures while a snowman and two more snowflakes were practising some steps in a corner.

One of the mothers noticed she was there.

``How is it?'' Miss Streete enquired.

``Fine,'' she answered.

``About five minutes,'' said Lara. ``I'll come and get them myself. OK?''

``Yes, they're all fed and watered,'' laughed the mother. And firmly securing an elastic band on the end of the plait, she said, ``There you are, Abigail; is that all right now?'' and the little girl nodded with solemn eyes.

Lara did the round of the other dressing-rooms and then returned to the main one.

``OK, Jenny?'' she asked. ``We're off again.''

Jenny nodded, her mouth so full of hairpins she couldn't speak.

Kathy came in. ``I've got it,'' she said triumphantly to Lara and she waved the wand at her.

``Annabel, are you ready for Joanna's quick change?'' Lara asked.

``Yes,'' said Annabel, ``I've got the clothes here,'' and she indicated a little pile of objects on the shelf behind her.

Lara went to get the children for the snow scene, and then they were off again.

Pictures of the performances she had appeared in flitted like ghosts through her mind. Alice had always had some lovely ideas for dances. And dressed the children beautifully.

She had an eye for a subtlety of colour that Lara knew eluded her. And because she had been a pupil at Alice's school for a fair number of years she had had some lovely parts. She remembered being an Edwardian lady, a Swiss maid complete with long blond plaits, a china doll, a cat, and her starring role as Princess Aurora. She remembered how she had got wind of this accolade, when Alice had said to her during a class ``And you will have to practise falling asleep.'' She remembered the steps she had been given and, when several years ago she had made the same ballet for the pupils of her own school, she had used the self-same steps for the `Rose Adagio' as she had had to do, out of a kind of homage to her former teacher. To her chagrin, when Alice came to the performance she didn't recognise them.

She had had many teachers since, but no one was more important in her eyes than Alice. She had weathered her adolescent storms, she had understood when she announced she couldn't dance if her mother was watching, she had taught her how to place a *jeté*, she had monitored her on her first pair of *pointe* shoes, she had fielded her desperate moans about the onset of menstruation. Most of all she had planted a picture in Lara's mind, an image that she had been pursuing all her life. Not as a dance teacher, mind you, but as that frail fairy-like creature that was a ballerina. When Alice had shown her a step or marked out an *enchaînement*, she became the dancer herself, performing and moving with self-absorption, tracing the pattern of her body into heart-achingly wonderful shapes, her arms and head held in that subtle tension that demands attention of the watcher.

Lara watched her own pupils from the wings, peeping through the dark curtains at the glare of the stage. They were acting out the odd and compelling story of the Snow Queen. Lara had taken a leaf out of another librettist's book and had merged the story of the *Baiser de la Fée*, the kiss of the fairy, with the Hans Andersen fairy tale. The Snow Queen had become an immortal figure, captivated by the beauty and innocence of a young boy who is enchanted with her wintry world. She claims him with a kiss in his youth and then, when he is about to marry his childhood sweetheart, Gerda, she arrives at the ceremony and takes him away to her snow palace. However, by the time Gerda has pursued him to the wintry wastes the Snow Queen has all but lost interest in him and Kay and Gerda are happily reunited, her loyal tears melting the ice that has settled round his heart. But the Snow Queen has already seen another little boy playing in the snow, and marked him as her own.

The binding kiss whereby she enchants Kay was the explanation for Liam's rosy sleeve.

'What an odd myth!' she thought as the snowflakes whirled faster and faster on the stage, threatening to dislodge the snowman's top hat. And yet it worked, it made Kay's hitching his sledge to the back of her sleigh quite plausible, like hitching one's wagon to a star. She watched as the dance moved to its climax, the Snow Queen, eyes glittering, dazzling the little boy by her beauty while he moved ever closer to her in a trance. She knew so clearly what the dance should look like that the action on the stage and the action in her head had become completely fused. When she divorced herself from her inner vision and viewed the action with the director's eye, she knew that neither Liam nor Kathy who were playing the parts had ingested the characters they were playing. She knew she could only give them the moves; the feeling had to come from somewhere inside them. Her good performers could take this imaginative leap and from their own dreams recreate hers. She had talked Kathy and Liam through the drama and explained what was going on, but although they tried, they skated along the surface of the action, never immersing themselves in the dangerous depths. On their own the moves were separate and empty, waiting for the characters' emotions and dramas to inhabit them. But she knew she was asking too much. How could they, she asked herself, understand this bizarre cycle of frozen love and obsession?

She contented herself with knowing what she wanted it to be, and deliberately chose to see it as it ought to be.

For how could they know about being in thrall? The acolyte and goddess enclosed in rapturous silent communion? And how had she herself arrived at its meaning? Why was it she saw the action as being in some meaningful way pivotal to her life and dancing?

She thought of Jeremy, the lover she had lost to a goddess more cruel and possibly more kind than the icy breaker of hearts. She had never stood rapt in front of him, bemused, captured and yet a willing sacrifice. Their partnership was an exploring of new ways, an opening up of life, not blinkered imprisonment, where passion was frozen and life and love locked out.

Flooded by the follow-spot, the besequinned elongated fingers of the fairy took the little boy's face in her hands and, gazing at it with a wild fierceness she tilted it towards her. She stooped forward slightly and kissed him seriously on his forehead. They froze. The curtain closed swiftly.

Liam came quickly into the wings and lifted his arm to wipe away the condemning smudge of lipstick.

``Got you,'' said his mother; she caught Lara's glance and they both laughed.

A few groups of people were waiting in the bar at the front of the theatre. Lara smiled as she recognised some of her former pupils. They chatted about what they were doing and then she passed on to a table where one of her oldest friends was sitting with her mother and daughters.

``Wonderful, as usual,'' her friend's mother said.

Lara smiled. She asked the girls if they had enjoyed it and how they were doing at their ballet school, what exams they were working for and what were their favourite dances. Then she moved towards the bar. There was a tray of drinks for the backstage helpers and she helped distribute them, leaving Jenny's as she still hadn't appeared, and taking a couple to Annabel and her boyfriend who were sitting huddled in a corner.

Then she saw Alice and sat down at the table. Richard gave her a kiss.

``Thanks for bringing your mum,'' she said. ``I should think you're a bit fed up with all this dancing lark, aren't you?'' she asked.

``Lara,'' he said, mock solemnly, ``what would my life be without it?''

``He's very versatile, you know,'' said Alice. ``He did the lights on my last show, and the sound on the one before that.''

``She'll have you on dancing, you know,'' laughed Lara.

``Oh, don't mention it. I did my stint before I was old enough to put up a good fight.''

``You loved every minute of it,'' Alice said, ``you know you did.''

``And are the girls following in the family tradition then?'' Lara asked, and was regaled with the activities of the little girls who stopped drawing on their straws and coca cola to tell her of their latest successes.

Alice leant forward. ``Come here, Nikki,'' she said. ``Let me wipe your nose.''

Lara remembered how strange it had at first seemed that her teacher could have a life that was independent of the dancing school, that she could engage herself in activities as mundane and earth-bound as cooking and changing nappies. The first time Lara had been to Alice's house had been on the occasion of a dancing examination. A few of her pupils were going to the Academy to take a grade exam and Alice had offered to deliver the children herself. Lara watched appalled as the lady that existed in her mind as a sylph broke eggs and fried them. The misery she endured at the shattering of this illusion quite mitigated whatever nervousness she was feeling about the exam. She came home and cried and cried and had no way of explaining to her surprised parents why. They put it down to the anxiety of taking the exam, and Lara couldn't bear to make the agony worse by putting it into words. It was bad enough as a feeling, as an idea, but to crystallize it with sentences was more than she had the stamina to do.

Equally, she had never been comfortable when she stayed with Alice. On the occasion of the production of *The Sleeping Beauty* she had spent a few days at her home. It had enabled her parents to take a short holiday together and meant that Alice could get her costume made with her alongside to try it on and coach her through some of the more difficult solos. Alice had had Richard by then and seeing her change his nappies and feed him his tea was another devastating experience for Lara.

``Have you got any you might try for JAs this year?'' Alice asked.

``No,'' Lara replied.

She had in the past tried to get a couple of her pupils, by becoming Junior Associates, onto the very first rung of the ladder for entry to the Royal Ballet School, but she had not yet been successful. The standards demanded were so exacting. Many were called, as they say, but few chosen.

``I've got one,'' said Alice. ``Oh, you should see her, Lara. Wonderful; leg up here.'' She shot her arm in the air and straightened it somewhere up by her ear.

Lara laughed. She remembered this was the way Alice had always demanded they should do their *developpés à la seconde*, with their legs somewhere in the stratosphere.

``She's lovely,'' Alice continued. ``Well, you'll see when you come to the next show.''

``I thought there wasn't going to be a next show,'' Lara said teasingly.

``No, truthfully,'' said Alice, peeved. ``She's good, isn't she?'' she appealed to Richard.

``Oh, you know Lara, Mum's latest,'' he said ruefully.

Lara remembered then how Alice certainly had had her enthusiasms, her favourite pupils. Not that she was unfair, but there was usually one amongst her pupils with whom she had a special *rapport*,who acted as the muse for her creativity and around whom she would build a dance or a ballet, using their especial talents as a springboard for her ideas.

`I suppose I was that once,' Lara suddenly thought, and realised with a sudden flash of insight how she must have been viewed by the other pupils at Alice's school. `Once, when I was a little girl I was the one who found favour in the eyes of this woman. And then it passed.' And she remembered being told of the exploits of her successors once she had gone on to another ballet school, not without the twinge of the displaced.

Now she was able to laugh; Alice was entirely predictable, age had changed her not a whit.

``The next Fonteyn, eh Mum?'' said Richard, with a gleam in his eye.''

Alice could not sense that she was being ribbed.

``No, honestly, Lara,'' she said, ``she is simply beautiful,'' and she brought her thumb and forefinger together in an elegant little well-remembered gesture.

``Well, you know,'' Alice continued, ``you think of giving
it all up, and for heaven's sake at my age I should have
retired years ago, and then a child comes to your school and
you see they have got, well, what it takes . . . and you decide
you can't. Don't you?''

``You're right,'' said Lara, ``and that's why we'll be in
harness until we die.''

Liam and Sibyl came up to their table. ``We've just come
to say goodnight and thank you,'' Sibyl said, leaning over and
touching Lara on the sleeve.

``Oh, thank you,'' said Lara quickly, standing up.

``I'll take it home and try to get it out in the wash,'' said
Sibyl, referring to the sleeve of Liam's shirt. ``Perhaps if I soak
it overnight it'll budge.''

``Oh, I shouldn't worry too much about it,'' said Lara, ``it's
only got one more performance to do, and it's not really all
that noticeable.''

As she stood up, so did Alice. ``Lara,'' she said, ``I won't
keep you from your guests. We've really enjoyed it. These
two'' – she indicated her grand-daughters with an embracing
gesture – ``have quite fallen for him.'' And she nodded her
grey eyes in the direction of Liam, who was well within
earshot.

Lara looked at him as he gave a sheepish grin and
blushed.

``You're breaking hearts all round,'' said Miss Streete
mock-sternly at him, only increasing, as she knew she would,
his confusion.

``It was a super show. Well done,'' continued Alice,
pulling on a pair of gloves and rearranging the mink collar on
her coat.

``Come on girls, Richard. Oh, have you my bag, Richard?''

``Of course I have,'' he said, giving Lara a long-suffering

look and a grin. ``Bye, Lara. Wonderful evening and you look younger every time I see you.'' He gave her a generous kiss.

Alice leaned forward and Lara embraced her fondly. ``Thank you again for coming,'' she said.

``Well, I expect I'll see you at the next. Give me a ring sometime.''

Lara nodded. Alice and her entourage moved towards the door of the bar. At the very last moment Alice turned and suddenly turning on the dance-school principal-superstar image, gave everyone in the bar a dazzling smile. Those who had been watching the departure felt warmed, and settled back happily into their conversations.

Sibyl and Liam, who had dropped back slightly to make way for the others to get out from their table, re-formed round Lara.

Jenny put her head round the door. ``D'you want a lift, Sibyl?'' she asked.

``Oh, please,'' said Sibyl.

``Well, I'm just off then,'' said Jenny.

``You have a drink here,'' said Lara, and lifted a glass from the tray on the bar.

``Oh, all right then,'' said Jenny. She sat down at the table Alice had vacated and Sibyl and Liam sat next to her.

``I'm going to try soaking the shirt overnight,'' Sibyl confided to Jenny.

Lara looked round the bar and seeing everyone in relatively deep conversation sat down again and reached for her glass of wine.

She recalled Alice saying on one occasion ``I've known this girl for more years than I care to remember.'' Sometimes it seemed like that, too; aeons and aeons, woven as Alice was into the long tortuous years of her childhood, almost as though there wasn't a time when she had not been there, or

Lara hadn't had that dream image in her head of a ballerina.

``Oh well,'' she heard Jenny say to Liam, ``you have only to be kissed one more time by Kathy and then it's all over.''

And she thought to herself `No, you only have to be kissed once and it's never over,' and her imagination flew to the small figure who was even now hurrying into her car outside the theatre.

Riding the Dragon

THERE were small clumps of teenagers, faces wiped green by the lights of the amusement arcade, standing washed up, bereft, outside. Miss Pruett glanced down at her nephew's face. His eyes shone and grew wider in the light. There was the jingle of falling coins and the electronic bleepings and whirring of the fruit machines within.

She was uncertain whether it had been such a good idea to bring him with her while she would be visiting her sister in what was obviously a terminal illness. She swallowed a little and hugged her purse handbag to her side a trifle protectively.

Her brother had promised Irene, his wife, that she would accompany him on his next business trip, and she was eager to see Amsterdam and have the break away. One son was staying with his grandmother, the other Miss Pruett had offered to bring to the seaside with her. The guest house was comfortably vacant, the season having hardly started. She forbore to stay at Sylvie's little almshouse; it was cramped and she was slightly uneasy about the legality of it. Furthermore, Oliver would not have been comfortable on the floor, even for the few days of his half-term holiday. She would put him on a train at the end of the holiday and stay on until the end if it were necessary.

Suddenly the place thudded with the noise of loud rock music; the lights dipped and flashed, the air pulsated with the

throb of drum beats. Orange and green, the lights burst out
over the sea front and twinkled their way across the sea to the
pacific boats moored quietly in the inky pool of the bay
beyond.

Oliver looked at her under curling eyelashes. ``Do you
really want to come in here, Aunty?'' he asked, not quite
believing it himself.

It had not after all been such a good idea, she decided,
having him with her. They had sat together on the beach and
she had bought him ice creams; they had been to the cinema
together and he had explained about light sabres and Jedi and
Ben-Kenobi. And while she made her dutiful visits to the
cottage hospital, he was happy to visit the library or walk to
the lighthouse and watch the fulmars wheeling in the newly
washed spring sky.

``Yes, of course,'' she said manfully. ``I want to see you
play the game you said you discovered here yesterday.''

``Do you want a go?'' he asked.

``I'll see about that,'' she said carefully, keeping her
options slightly open.

The kids sauntered away in slight bursts of movement,
laughing rather obviously and watching each other carefully
as they tested their newly-found sense of each other. Girls
watched covertly under their eyelids as boys sprawled
nonchalantly over the kids' mini-roundabout. More groups of
boys walked by, casually stretching their throats and arching
their backs while the night breeze stirred currents in their
blood that disturbed and frightened them.

``What was it called again?'' she asked.

``Star Warrior,'' he said. ``I'll pay. I've still got plenty of
the pocket money Mum and Dad gave me.''

``All right, then.''

She launched herself into the swirling, whirling palace of

fun. The sound broke around her like a wave breaking on the beach. The carpet under her feet felt soft and decadent to her tread. The noises splattered and dappled her. People stood in rapt communication with machines, attention riveted to the screens in front of them, pushing buttons, winding wheels, pulling joy-sticks back and forth. A couple of girls pushed passed them laughing, open and rumpled, a bag of chips in one of their hands, wide mouths grinning.

Oliver threaded his way to the cash desk where he exchanged his money for some change. He made his way quickly and unerringly to the machine, leading Miss Pruett past the hunched shoulders of the game players.

``Oh,'' he said, ``we'll have to wait. There is someone already on it.''

He indicated a cockpit-shaped crevice where an older boy sat, his face stencilled with lines and starbursts. All around the air sang and throbbed, whilst Roman candles of light burst red spangles on Oliver's face.

``We'll wait,'' he said. ``He won't be long.''

So they stood where Oliver could watch the other boy glide through a dizzy universe of starships and enemy spacecraft.

``How on earth do you know what to do?'' Miss Pruett asked. ``It all seems to go so quickly.''

``Oh, you learn,'' he said, with the easy assurance of the young. Miss Pruett, who had trouble even with Oliver's pocket calculator, wondered whether his facility would now elude her.

Oliver's face went puce and then a pale lime green. The hue reminded her, in its ghastliness, of Sylvie's pale and tortured face. The wasted and slightly twisted body, the shrivelled flesh and the bitter grin on her mouth. She had never been easy. Considerably older than either Miss Pruett or her brother, she had lived a life of taut disappointment. Although neither of them had married, Miss Pruett had come to terms with her single status; she lived a life that exacted as much as she put into it. She played the piano at Miss Streete's dancing school, she sang in the choral society, she went to the opera, and with her friend Audrey occasionally attended the local *thé dansant*. With her father's small legacy she had visited Greece, and every so often would go to the ballet. Sylvie had moved herself away to the sea, where after a lifetime of being a librarian she had immersed herself in books. On a couple of occasions she had invited Miss Pruett to stay with her. She extolled the delights of being beside the sea and yet, once Miss Pruett had taken up residence, seemed to set great store by making life unpleasant for her. On those occasions Miss Pruett had gone to bed to cry gently for some hours after unsuccessfully fielding some of the sharp hurtful things that Sylvie had said. Although she was reluctant to admit it, she had to acknowledge that this visit to the seaside was considerably more pleasant without Sylvie's difficult and unnerving day-to-day presence.

Oliver nudged her.

``It's free,'' he whispered. She watched as the young boy vacated the cabin and Oliver shot into his place and put his money into the slot. She watched breathlessly as he appeared to be hurtling through space, shifting and lurching as the ship changed angle. Stars and whirling flying saucers came rushing at him from nowhere. There was an extraordinary score number in one corner of the screen, and the digits flew up in their thousands. Suddenly the screen cleared.

``Oh dear,'' she said, ``is that it?''

``Oh no,'' he said. ``I've gone to a different level.''

She nodded sagely.

``Is that good?'' she asked.

``Of course,'' he replied. And off he was again, this time flying his way through huge obelisks that swung towards him from the horizon in a matter of seconds. Miss Pruett felt slight vertigo. Then it was all over. The screen went black and white, then orange. Suddenly there was a huge snaking dragon worming its way across the screen.

``Ooh-er,'' said Oliver, and swung himself about in his seat.

The dragon lunged and lurched at him, breathing a stream of fire in his direction. There was a great burst of flame and he was consumed.

``Game over,'' the screen announced.

``Good, isn't it?'' he said as he climbed out. ``I'd never got that far before.''

``You'd never seen that dragon?'' she asked breathlessly.

``No,'' he said. ``I'm not very good at fighting that. I lost all my lives in about three milliseconds.''

``Mmm . . . '' she said. She had little to offer by way of advice.

``Would you like a go?'' he asked.

``Um. Well perhaps not tonight,'' she said; ``it all seems rather fast.''

She thought playing the hornpipe for the Grade Twos was about as breakneck as she was able to go without her body and bones disintegrating. This game made the dance almost sedate by comparison.

``Do you want another go?'' she asked.

``Tomorrow perhaps,'' he said, hesitating a little.

``I'll give you some money for it,'' she conceded.

So they left the hall of delights, with its screams and thunderous music and let the soothing embrace of the gentle sea calm them down as they walked the fringe of the bay to their lodgings.

There was a call in the morning. Miss Sylvie Pruett had regained her speech to a degree and was anxious to see her sister. Miss Pruett said she would be along immediately.

``I'll meet you in the corner café at lunch time, Oliver,'' she said; ``say one o'clock? I'll join you there. You will be all right, dear?''

``Yes, of course,'' he said. ``With these binoculars I can see very clearly. I saw some shearwaters last time. I'll look for them again.''

He gave her one of his lop-sided grins.

``I wonder whether this is much of a holiday for you,'' she said apologetically.

``I'm having a really fab time,'' he said.

She hesitated.

``Honestly,'' he said, with open childish guile.

And she was inclined to believe him.

Sylvie lay at the end of the ward, her white face the colour of the white sheets. Miss Pruett approached the bed, a bunch of white carnations in her arms. She felt as blanched as their petals. The sister came up to her.

``You understand, her speech is not at all clear,'' she explained.

Miss Pruett nodded.

``It's probably got to her brain, you see. But she is almost intelligible. You will probably understand her better than we can.''

Miss Pruett stared.

``I'll find a vase for the flowers,'' said the sister. ``Stay as long as you like. I'll be in my office at the end of the ward if you want me.''

Miss Pruett still stood motionless.

``She's not suffering, dear, you know that,'' the sister

reassured; ``and – well – it can't be too long now.''

Miss Pruett nodded again and then pulling herself together, turned and gave the sister her kind smile. The sister went out.

``Sylvie,'' Miss Pruett said, and then sat on the chair at the bedside.

The face turned, and the eyes very slowly opened. ``Clara? . . . You fool,'' croaked the strange voice. ``You fool.''

Miss Pruett waited.

``You always wasted yourself . . . you wasted your talent . . . now you are wasting your time here . . . you always were a stupid, sentimental fool.''

Miss Pruett gulped and listened. The voice continued. Past prejudices, judgments and condemnations were uttered. The fabric of her life was being torn at by someone determined to reduce her tranquillity to rage, to see her in tatters. She swallowed hard.

``I'll be gone soon and you'll be saddled with your wasted, useless life,'' it went on.

Miss Pruett listened. Sylvie was having the last word.

She emerged from the hospital in a daze. The sunlight struck her and she blundered her way down the hill towards the town.

Oliver was waiting for her.

She ordered lunch and, when it came, played with her Welsh rarebit.

Oliver consumed two banana splits and told her about the kittiwake colony he had been watching, enthusing about their plumage and the clever shape of their eggs. Then he said ``You'll never guess what!''

``What?'' she said dully, sipping her tea to dislodge the toast that seemed dry in her mouth.

``I've conquered the dragon!''

``Oliver!'' she said. ``You didn't waste a lot of your money in that amusement arcade?''

He looked hurt at the reprimand.

``Well, no, not *wasted*,'' he emphasised; ``I learnt how to deal with the dragon.''

`Cunning child,' thought Miss Pruett, `he's palmed off his visit as a learning experience. It's extraordinary how children manage to handle adults. He's not a dull boy,' she concluded, and sighed a little.

``D'you want to see?''

She hesitated.

``Or shall I tell you?''

``No,'' she smiled. ``No. You show me, Oliver.''

So she settled the bill and they went along the sea front to the amusement arcade.

The game was free so Oliver went to sit at the controls. She put two ten pence pieces in the slot and he was away. The same dizzy array that she had watched the preceding night swung into action. Oliver rolled and twisted and fought his way through the interstellar battlefield. Then the dragon appeared.

``Watch!'' he carolled.

With one leap he jumped his space warrior onto the back of the dragon and from there fought off the fire of the invading alien craft.

She watched amazed.

He proceeded from level to level, and then finally, as before, his powers were of no more use and the game was over.

``Have you won?'' she said breathlessly.

``No, of course not. There're about two billion levels in there anyway, but that's as far as I've managed to get so far.''

She looked at him with pride.

``Good, isn't it? You have to ride the dragon, you see.''

``I noticed,'' she said.

The next day at the hospital Sylvie continued her final bitter vituperations.

``Life's a miserable waste of time, Clara,'' she said. ``You'll find that out. You'll be left like me, alone and friendless. Just you wait and see.''

``Yes, dear,'' said Miss Pruett.

``Dear nothing!'' Sylvie retorted. ``You've never liked me, so don't pretend. But then, all your life's been a pretence, hasn't it?''

``Yes,'' she murmured, ``I expect you're right.''

``You only come and see me out of a stupid sense of duty . . .''

``Yes,'' she conceded, ``you always were so right.''

``And you'll be glad when I'm gone – don't try to deny it!''

``I shall be glad for both of us,'' she concurred.

``Well, don't worry,'' Sylvie muttered. ``I won't keep you long.''

``No, not long now,'' she echoed.

``And then,'' Sylvie rambled on, not to be outdone, ``you can drag out your own miserable existence with a clear conscience . . .''

``How well you understand me – have always understood me,'' purred Miss Pruett, almost light-headed with complicity.

Sylvie died two days later, replete with her rightness, content that she had at last made Clara see her point of view and shed her ridiculous pretences.

``Before we go, Aunty,'' Oliver said, ``do you want to have a go of Space Warrior?''

``Not really, dear,'' she found herself saying; ``I've already learnt how to ride the dragon,'' and she smiled at him.

``It's been a good holiday,'' he said; ``I'm glad you're coming home on the train with me.''

``So am I,'' she said.

Lady Luck

IN the dark corridor James's mother stood clutching a jersey. Miss Streete, one ear attuned to the music creeping under the closed doors of the church hall – assigned as examination room for the day – heard the loo flush and caught her anxious glance.

``He says he mucked it all up.''

James emerged, a small hunched figure in white T-shirt, black tights and shoes and white socks.

Miss Streete looked at him. ``What happened, James?'' she asked.

``I just wobbled all the time,'' James complained. ``Every time I stood on one leg, I wobbled. The arabesque was awful.''

Lara looked at him and smiled. ``I don't suppose it was nearly as bad as you think,'' she reassured him. ``Then I mucked up all the *enchainements*,'' he growled, and, hanging his head, disappeared back into the gents.

Miss Streete looked at his mother.

``I think he's more cross with himself than anything else,'' she confided.

``I expect you're right,'' Lara agreed and then, hearing the strains of the curtsey music, moved quickly back into the kitchen.

``Next two,'' she called. ``Becky and Charlotte, are you ready?''

Two prim little figures moved towards her, two pairs of

eyes scanned her face anxiously.

``Have you got your report papers?'' she said, knowing the question to be superfluous, because she could see them clutched in each girl's hand.

The candidates nodded mutely.

``Follow me,'' she said and smiled and led them to the closed hall doors.

The darkness of the corridor was quenched by a burst of light – the door opened and two leotarded girls emerged, their eyes bright and faces pink with exercise. They dashed past the waiting group into the kitchen.

``When you give her the report papers, give her a nice smile and a curtsey and say `Good morning, Miss Sutcliffe','' Miss Streete instructed.

``Mrs Sutcliffe?'' asked Becky.

``No, _Miss_ Sutcliffe,'' Lara corrected, ``and don't forget to point your toes all the time and smile . . .'' She looked up and caught the figure of Becky's mother emerging from the kitchen door.

``Enjoy it, Becky love,'' she called, her face white with anxiety and her eyes anticipating something far from pleasure.

Lara heard the bell and with a whispered ``good luck'' opened the door and watched the girls walk into the room. She closed the door and, catching Becky's mother's eye, said ``She'll be fine – commended at the very least,'' and laughed.

Becky's mother went back into the kitchen as James emerged from the loo in his outdoor clothes; from the hall the piano notes swooped into the music for _pliés_.

``I've never wobbled so much, Miss Streete,'' the little boy complained, ``and I bet she noticed.''

``She knows people wobble, James,'' Lara explained. ``She's danced herself, you know – and people don't fail exams just because of a bit of a wobble.''

``I think he's just cross with himself,'' his mother repeated philosophically.

James walked past her, his head hanging, his gait moody. Lara could not but watch him with amusement – she loved him for his vehemence.

``Don't let him be too hard on himself – he's doing wonderfully,'' she said.

``Yes,'' the mother laughed and agreed, and followed her huffy son out of the church hall.

Lara remembered when he had arrived together with his younger sister. Their mother and father had been there, too, and the mother had said``Tell Miss Streete why you want to dance, James.''

``Because Daddy did,'' James had replied.

Lara had looked at the father with renewed respect. ``That's wonderful,'' she said, ``you must have enjoyed it if you're encouraging your son.''

``Oh yes,'' he replied and gave her a boyish smile.

And James had made conspicuous progress, fortunate in that his parents encouraged him – similarly talented boys often did not have such luck. Miss Streete always admired her boy pupils; they were invariably outnumbered by the girls and she saw in them a rare quality of persistence and courage. Despite the dash and energy of Morris dancing, English culture did not look happily on men dancing – Scottish, Greek, Spanish, Eastern European, Russian, African, Indian, Australian Aborigine and Polynesian cultures all embraced both sexes in joyous movement – but ballet, although it had been instituted by a more than virile king and some of its greatest exponents were male, was still considered slightly suspect. Sometimes she was provoked into pointing out that the physical demands of ballet required considerable strength and athleticism and when the inevitable pronouncements followed that all male dancers were gay, she'd try to reason that there were gay pilots, gay dentists, gay solicitors. Any child or his parent weathering a degree of social hostility had her immediate and lasting admiration. It was beginning to get better – but there was a great deal of prejudice and circumspection still. Gracefulness seemed to be less and less of a desirable human attribute she realised: perhaps it was grace itself that was the problem. There had been a distinct move away from grace and even graciousness from some time before the First World War. Certainly, few men nowadays aspired to gracefulness. Wondering why, she decided to leave the reasoning to social anthropologists. But that was why she treasured her boy pupils – why they became immediately, despite herself, her particular pets, not just for their rarity, but for their dogged vocational courage. Her heart went out to James.

Just as she was returning to the kitchen, another little girl arrived. ``Change and leave all your clothes in the ladies loo, Gemma,'' she said, ``then come in here.''

Jenny was twisting a child's hair into a bun and then, shielding her eyes from the spray, was applying a liberal layer of lacquer to the escaping wisps of a fringe. ``I'm fighting the battle of the fringe again here,'' she laughed, her voice muffled because she was holding several hair-clips in her mouth.

``I'll put the kettle on,'' said Lara. ``We'll give her,'' and with a nod of her head towards the rooms she indicated the examiner,``another cup of coffee after Becky and Charlotte; and I don't know about you, but I could do with one too.'' She moved to the sink and filled the kettle and then, pushing aside several hair-bands and hair-nets stood waiting for it to boil.

The next three candidates were practising spring *pointes*

whilst their mothers were in earnest conversation. Miss Streete looked at the children's sleek classical hair styles and shining pink satin shoes and ribbons. Then she ran her eyes down the list of candidates, noting who had arrived, checking their times against her list, checking names and fees.

She glanced at her watch, listened again to the music issuing from the hall and commented ``She's keeping pretty much to time.'' Then as she listened she heard the music repeat, and then repeat again. ``Oh dear,'' she said, as much to herself as to anyone who might be listening; ``seems they're having several shots at the polka,'' and wondered at turned-in knees, unpointed toes, feet not joining in third, movements going in wrong directions.

``Is that bad?'' asked one of the mothers.

``Not as bad as them declaring they've never been taught it,'' smiled Lara. ``Oh, don't look so surprised,'' she added. ``I've had pupils in exams roundly declare they've never seen a *petit jeté*, or heard of an *attitude* or a *sissone ouverte* – let alone been taught it.''

The mothers all laughed, grateful for an excuse to relieve the tension.

Lara had never forgotten the mother who announced that on the day before the exam she had dreamt that the pupils were not to do the exam but the mothers had to go and be examined instead. She well understood this anxiety – because, in effect, she was being examined. Each session she held – and over the years she'd held dozens – she knew it was her teaching that was being scrutinised, and if her standards failed so would the pupils.

By way of distracting herself she made three coffees, one black for Jenny, two whites for herself and the examiner and tea for Miss Pruett, and then arranged some biscuits on a plate. ``Jenny,'' she asked, ``can you hold the door for me when the next lot come out? – and I'll take these in.''

``Mmm,'' Jenny answered, capturing a small head in a hair-net. ``Whereabouts are they?''

``The balletic variation I think,'' Lara said, listening again to the music coming from the hall.

When Becky and Charlotte were safely out and the coffee and biscuits safely in, Lara collapsed in a chair.

``Miss Streete,'' Becky said, ``she asked us to do a *pas de bourée devant* with the back foot.''

``Oh dear,'' said Lara. ``Well, what did you do?''

``I didn't know,'' Becky replied. ``I just stood there.''

``You goose – what did you do, Charlotte?''

Charlotte, who had already removed her ballet shoes, turned and looked at her shyly.

``Well, show me,'' Lara encouraged, standing up.

In her pink socks, Charlotte made some movements.

``Fine!'' Lara said. ``Well done! – Did you see, Becky? It's logical, isn't it? But I hadn't taught you that, I know – I think it's a bit complicated for your grade. I usually do all the *pas de bourées* with different feet with the grade fours and fives. Oh well –'' She sat down again. ``Tell Gemma and Jane to come here,'' she said to Becky. ``I'd better just check they know.''

``How many more Grade Threes?'' Jenny asked.

``These three,'' Lara indicated, ``then two Grade Fours and then lunch – ''

``I'll get the butter out,'' said Jenny. ``I usually forget and it's then so hard I can't spread it.''

``Except for the time you forgot it,'' laughed Lara.

``Oh yes – and then I couldn't think why the sandwiches kept falling apart. – There,'' she pushed a sleek candidate away from her; ``will that do?''

``Super,'' Lara enthused. ``Gosh, I only ever see you all

looking like ballerinas when we do exams.''

Mrs Grant (more than usually flustered) presented herself suddenly with her daughter at the kitchen door. ``Susan's only brought her old ballet shoes,'' she announced, exasperated. ``I'll kill her,'' she added cheerfully.

Susan looked up with languid eyes.

``I've got some here,'' said Jenny, and immediately she started rummaging in a large plastic carrier bag. ``What size is she?''

``Five,'' Mrs Grant replied. ``Honestly I'll kill her,'' she reiterated. ``I really will.''

``I'll cut some ribbon,'' Lara said. ``We'll have to get a move on – that's *assemblés* they're doing –``

``I've bought new ones,'' Mrs Grant complained, ``and she decides to leave them at home,'' – and together with Jenny she starts hurriedly sewing the ribbons to the shoes.

Frantic minutes pass.

``Highland Fling!'' says Lara helpfully, and Jenny shoots her a glance. ``But she does quite a lot of writing after they come out,'' she adds.

The ribbons are attached, the new shoes tied into place with neat reef knots on the inside of the ankle and, breathlessly, Susan and her fellow candidate delivered to the examination room. Miss Streete and Jenny look at each other.

``I bet you really enjoy this,'' Mrs Grant says, smiling broadly.

``And how,'' Lara says, feigning a faint, leaning back in her chair.

At lunch Miss Pruett comes out into the kitchen and conversationally supposes that they have all done all right, so far. And she recounts who has made the examiner laugh, who has kept cool whilst her fellow candidate has suddenly gone to pieces, who knew all their French terms, who has and who has not acquitted themselves with honour.

Lara always bowed to Clara's experience when it came to this analysis. Although she was absorbed in playing the music, Miss Pruett had a very deft eye for the talents and performances of the children. Lara appreciated again what an asset she was – either engaging the examiner in conversation or remaining discreetly uninvolved. On one occasion she had even sprung from her chair and caught an Elementary candidate who was fainting.

The session moved into the afternoon and, as the examinations became longer, so the traffic in and out of the kitchen slowed. The older candidates arrived without a retinue of parents, siblings and friends, and rather than practising *glissades* in the corridor, sat in quiet corners studying their syllabuses. However, the longer the sessions, the pinker the faces of the returning examinees. Clutching their *pointe* shoes, the Elementary candidates entered the room at the insistent dinging of the bell. They were the last entrants for the day.

Jenny started gathering up hair pins and head-bands; Lara, chewing idly on a biscuit, ran the hot water to wash the dishes. She sighed – well, the day was nearly over – with luck they would all pass. She'd had very few failures over the years – but there had been the occasional anomaly – the odd rogue mark, erring as much on the side of extra merit as failure. She'd been as surprised by the odd candidate achieving honours as she had by one not passing – and these she supposed, ruefully, cancelled each other out. But no! It wasn't luck – there was too often a consistency between her mental markings and the examiners' mark.

Luck was something entirely iniquitous – it was luck that brought certain talents to people, luck that brought certain pupils to her classes, luck that took Jeremy away, brought Annabel and Clara Pruett their latest job; luck that shattered her knee, luck that bestowed short Achilles tendons and natural turnout. Luck flew in the face of human endeavour and aspiration, picked up some, hurled down others.

She swirled the washing-up liquid round the bowl. It had been a long day and she felt very drained of energy. She thought of some of her fellow college students who had become fêted ballerinas and subsequently made happy, successful marriages and led comfortable lives in their retirement. Comparing what she knew of their and her life styles made her sigh. How was it some people were so utterly blessed while others had to deal with strings and strings of disappointments? Was it only in the arts, she wondered. No, of course not – every field had its successes and failures. She knew also that the crumb of comfort that most people clasped desparately to themselves was that on average things evened up, balanced. But in her heart she doubted it. Today parents, candidates and herself would all suffer a bit, to a lesser or greater degree, from nerves, and when they found they had passed, would be happy. That seemed like a fair equation – but overall, life was not so fair. Luck seemed to be the random factor. Luck that flies in the face of credibility, luck which throws off balance or redresses it violently.

Thinking of balance, she thought of James again – cross because he'd lost his in his arabesque. One of the feats of dancing was balancing – holding a position on one leg, one toe even, defying nature. There were parts in the `Rose Adagio' and the `Black Swan' *Pas de Deux* when the whole house drew breath as the ballerina left all support and held a position for as long as she could, defying gravity and speculation. In an unfair world she was making a defiant gesture – and so we admire it – admire it because it is unnatural – in a way that nature, which includes men's lives, is not.

Jenny started adding up the money as Lara dried up the crockery and then started storing the food back in Jenny's ice-bag.

``You'll take the biscuits, won't you Jenny?'' she asked her, twinkling.

``There you go again,'' Jenny grumbled, ``leading me astray – with friends like you, who needs enemies, as they say.'' She put some money in an envelope and sealed it. ``This is Clara's money. – Are you taking the register home?''

``Probably,'' Lara said. ``– Did Mrs Grant pay for the shoes?''

``Yes – poor woman. That's two new pairs she's bought in less than a week. I don't think I've ever sewn on a pair of ribbons so quickly – ''

``All part of the fun,'' Lara said, and then added ``Well, at least you were here to do them securely. Nicky lost a ribbon last time, do you remember?''

``Because they were held in place with two stitches and the ends weren't turned under. Do you wonder at it –'' Jenny grumbled.

Then she started to stack some chairs and Lara, her ears suddenly pricking, ran from the kitchen to the doors of the hall. When she returned, she explained. ``Just checking Sarah's *pointe* work variation.''

``Oh, applying the eye to the draughty crack in the door?'' Jenny suggested. ``I always wonder why you never finish these sessions without a nasty attack of conjunctivitis.''

``I mostly resist the temptation,'' Lara said, ``and if I do look, I only see what I don't want to: knock-knees and sickled toes.''

``Was she OK?''

``Mm, fine,'' Lara conceded.

``They'll all be OK,'' Jenny reassured.

Sure enough, when the fat envelope plopped onto Lara's door mat the following week and her anxious eyes had scanned the marks, they had indeed all passed. She looked for James's name in particular. The examiner, too, had looked with benevolence on her only boy pupil and, calling him a very promising candidate, had given him `Highly Commended'. Lara, nodding at the mild complicity, smiled to herself and allowed the briefest moment of self-congratulation; then, remembering the hours of patient tuition liberally laced with nagging and haranguing, conceded that luck had had nothing to do with it.

Lifting the Veil

WE crouch on the floor at Miss Streete's feet. She plays the sad music to us from her tape machine, and tells us the sad tale we are to enact in the dance. The music pours out its cold melancholy into the hall. I feel its rivulets seep through my shoulder-blades into me, flooding me like a lake behind a dam with anxiety, tension and apprehension.

She tells us to spread out, to find a space in the hall, to let the sadness out on the wings of the music – and dance.

Remove the stopper from the genie's bottle? – Does she know what she is asking? I have seen the smoke that pours out, the billowing enveloping clouds, black as death, rolling, rolling from the neck and tumbling over the ploughed and ordered fields and swamping the cities – and from the thickness of that murk the great hulk of a djinn rear like a cliff – his fearsomeness not so much in his size as in his power to identify desire, to feed appetite, to satiate want. Now as the music gathers itself to spring, she says `Let him free, show us unconstraint.' My head spins. I have the fear of the urge surging around me. My heart thud – thud – thuds in my ears, deafens me, starts to block out the music. The air of my breath is only just before my nose and it is as thick as blood.

How can I? Miss Streete's eyes are cool. Surely she too feels the pull of the great tides to and fro? The other girls look at each other, fear coruscating from their edges as from frost on leaves in autumn. Sophie gives a high giggle and Miss

142

Streete quietens her.

I feel despair in a gesture; I move my hand, heavy, low, down and away, as the mighty Archer wheels over my head; and a veil pulls and the pageant of suffering careers through my arteries; I am aflame with grief and still it rides through me, war-driven, disease-driven, curling and coiling about me.

Am I to let this free? It's not just the laughter – my terror is not that I might suffer a loss of face (although I might), but that I will confront the watchers with their own horror. And if they laugh then, when humility is the only acceptable response, then the thunderbolt will strike and they will be anathema. Why then do they watch at all?

The pity of the human condition, with its rapture and nobility, its joy and its sorrow: this is the great fecund area, the source of all myth and legend, of all fictions – where good and evil are balanced in the trembling human soul. Oh I can dance it, but will anyone really want to see it and acknowledge it?

Miss Streete's foot is tapping absently, lifting and falling within and without the music; her eyes are absent yet far-seeing, as she urges us to dance.

We scatter and fall on the floor, in little embryonic heaps. A mist seems to settle round my shoulders, a comforting veil, a comfortable shroud. I could wait down here, asleep, forever. My shyness chills me, a cloud before the sun; it is the fear of revealing the orb; the shield I hold up, not as a mirror to nature – more the mist on that mirror, which my dance will wipe away; it is both a rite and a statement.

Slowly I lift my limbs to the sky: my head, my neck, is stretched and pale as a young queen's before the executioner's axe falls. My arms extend and from them the lightning flows, out through my fingertips reaching to the far edges of the universe, where the galaxies wheel and tumble in chaotic motion. Now my legs move, urging my body forwards and backwards, screwed by the heavy, broad waters of the sea: riding the tempests, sweeping the surge of waves onto the shore. I am possessed and immolated and lose myself. I hear the music; I hear Miss Streete's commands; I spin the flexible fibres of my moving into a patterned strand of spirit-stuff.

But now I see my mother, her long grey coat casting frightened shadows into her blue eyes – and I see those eyes and I know that I have to stop. Fear and shame flood my face: for she saw me uncovered and I see the look of dread. She knows me now and knows I have knowledge. We kept this pretence of adult and child so perfectly when confined by the mundanity of home and hearth: now I know she knows I know the pain of parturition, the fear of the black things that creep behind doors in the middle of the night, the snarl of the tiger and the purple scar of passion. She, who tried to protect me from suffering, has seen what I never wanted her to see, that my vulnerability is my own and I have called it back to myself.

Too late I retreat into shyness. I relapse in a chair, panting slightly, tears blurring my vision. My mother shoots me a glance and the arrow impales me to the chair. She keeps her distance, divided from me by fear and embarrassment. But I still need her, her protection and love, and I despair of the distance I have created. I have trespassed too deeply into the mysteries: the dance and the music gave me the information – or perhaps they merely corroborated what I knew from birth? I had removed the stopper from the bottle, drawn aside the veil; I had lifted the lid from Pandora's box – and my mother had seen something which baffled and hurt her. It's a true and honest thing, but not the sort of thing she wanted to see, nor did I want her to see it. Is this where my shyness stems from? – from my wanting to protect my mother?

Miss Streete comes over and puts a hand on my huddled shoulder, the heat and energy of exercise still emanating from my body making clammy contact with her cool hands.

``It's all right,'' she says; and then slides her arm along my shoulder as the crying becomes sobs. ``I understand.'' And she looks up at my mother. She gently shakes her head. ``I too found it hard to dance in front of my mother.'' As she smiles my mother moves forward, and then sits heavily on a chair next to me.

``I thought you *enjoyed* dancing,'' she said.

``I do,'' I hiccoughed.

``If it's going to have this effect on you,'' she said, burying her concern in tartness, ``perhaps you shouldn't be doing it.''

I couldn't explain. She was saying something else, side-tracking. I shook my head and sniffled.

``And it is, after all, something you do in front of other people, isn't it? So if you're liable to dissolve in stage fright at any moment . . .'' She looked to Miss Streete for support.

Miss Streete made a non-committal noise: ``Mmm.'' Then she said ``Most of the time we are thinking of – we concentrate on what is being done – the steps, you know, the movements . . .'' She paused.

My mother looked from her to me. She nodded slightly and handed me a tissue.

I don't know whether the movement prevented her from hearing Miss Streete's next quiet words: `` – rather than what is being said.''

The Wedding

THE confetti flowered in the sunshine, a blizzard of blossom catching the golden light, caught by the wind swirling round the bride's veil, lifting it up and away and then hurling itself down the street. Lara threw another handful, then Trudi, her oldest friend, scuttled alongside her, and together they joined the crowd pelting the young couple.

Trudi's sister, Mina, heavily-hatted like a satin toadstool, confided ``I'm throwing plenty of rice, Trudi dear; I'm determined you'll be a grandma soon.''

Trudi turned and grinned then, catching the eye of a friend in the crowd, retreated towards the church, arms extended. Miss Streete threw caution and a lot more confetti to the wind.

Imogen, fielding her veil, laughed at her happily. ``I pointed my toes all the way up the aisle,'' she announced. ``I just hope you were looking.''

``No more than I expected, Imo,'' Lara retorted. Then, after a word from the photographer, Imogen and Bron, now her husband, carefully guided her billowing wedding dress into the limousine.

More photographs were taken under the trees in the grounds of the hotel where the reception was being held, with Imogen like a water-lily floating amongst the sea of colours and flowers. Lara noticed that Trudi still held herself like a dancer and, in her daring pink with matching shoes and a silly confection of feathers and net on her head, looked about seventeen.

She sidled up to Lara whose coat and dress were of a more demure dusty pink. ``Roll on the g and t's,'' she muttered *sotto voce*. ``It's been a long day and it's still not over.''

``Imo looks wonderful, Trudi,'' Lara said, ``and it's all going so well . . . ''

``Keep your fingers and toes crossed then,'' Trudi said. ``Problems?''

``Well – it's not been easy with Bron's parents . . . ''

``Oh yes,'' Lara remembered. ``Separated aren't they?''

Trudi took Lara's arm and indicated with her eyes to her husband that they were going indoors.``More than separated, overwhelmingly divided.''

Miss Streete looked at Bron, one arm round the waist of his bride and the other calming the clouds of netting veil – and then at his mother Naomi who stood under a red maple tree with Bron's brothers closely, protectively, on either side. She in her peacock blue and the dark-suited fair-headed young men formed a group against the ruby red maple leaves, glowing in the late summer sunshine.

Trudi recounted the details as they walked across the rain-softened grass, both of them tip-toeing carefully to avoid their heels sinking into the ground. Lara listened, head bowed.

She looked again at Imogen, now walking with Bron back to the hotel reception room, laughing with her father. Lara remembered her so well in her pale pink leotard, dark hair straying from her hair-band in damp tendrils, eyes fierce with concentration as she battled to lift her leg from fourth to second and maintain both height and turnout.

``You're lifting your hip, Imo,'' she would say, hesitating, because she had said it so many times before.

``I know,'' the girl would reply.

Miss Streete stood behind her and placed her hands on her

hips – pushing them *en face*.

``Start again, take the *developpé* slowly – good *retiré*, right
. . . ''

And Imogen's knuckles whitened as she hung desperately
onto the back of the chair.

``Keep it low . . . the height will come.''

Imogen's leg moved from in front slowly to the side.

``Keep the weight off your supporting leg,'' Lara urged;
``good, good, it's only practice,'' and she smiled at her and
then, noticing the clenched hand, said ``And of course a
dancer's hand only rests two finger-tips *lightly* on the *barre!*''
and all the class laughed because they knew it was one of
Miss Streete's favourite jokes, simply because so often it was
untrue.

At the end of the lesson Imo had said ``I don't think I'll
ever get my Grade Five. Let alone my Elementary; I just
haven't got the turn-out,'' and Lara knew it was true. Trudi,
too, knew it was true – she'd entrusted Lara with her
daughter's dancing since she was four, when she had
ambitions for her daughter to be a ballerina. After all, when
she herself left the college where she'd met Lara she'd gone
straight into the *corps de ballet* of The Festival Ballet. When Imo
made her unexpected appearance she married her father and
gave his acting career all her support. She used to say there
was only room for one star in the family and laughed off her
descent into domesticity, as she called it. But they were a
happy family and John had become a successful and well-
respected actor.

She had watched Imo have one of her first lessons with
Lara and then said to her ``She's got no turn-out, has she?''

Lara replied ``No, not much,'' and watched her friend sigh.

``Oh well,'' Trudi said, and Lara saw the pragmatic woman
she had become swim to the surface.

``But,'' said Lara, ``she dances wonderfully.''

``I know,'' Trudi confirmed. ``I've seen her doing her Isadora all round the sitting-room; I've seen her responding to music since she could first move. Must be John's genes . . . ''

Lara laughed. ``Do you want to stop the lessons?'' she asked.

``No – no, of course not. She loves it so and you're the best . . . ''

Lara gulped gratefully.

``Oh, come on,'' said Trudi, ``I know you never thought you'd teach. We were taught to consider it second best – but where on earth would any of us be without teachers? Even the mediocre ones, let alone the good ones. And you *are* a good one, Lara – you're a natural educator.''

As her friend gave her this bouquet Lara looked at her with grey eyes wide with gratitude and her mind reeled back quickly to all the other times Trudi had encircled her with the golden noose of friendship.

``With you Imo will maximise what dance talent she has – I know she will – and she'll enjoy doing so – she'll find her niche, I know she will, and if it's not to be dancing, well, it'll not be dancing.''

And Imogen did. With Lara's careful tuition and her own determination she had managed to pass her Elementary examination and then decided to train as a stage manager. At drama college she had done well, owing to her capacity for hard work and self-discipline – which Lara liked to think, if not acquired at her dancing lessons, certainly had been exercised there. And now that despairing pink-faced little girl was a young woman – having never lost the engaging mannerism of nodding her head as she smiled.

Now Imo took up her spoon. The wedding guests were all waiting for their cue – and so the wedding breakfast began.

Looking up at the high table, Lara's eye was caught by Trudi, who with a swift grimace directed her glance to Bron's father sitting next to her, bent over his melon cocktail. His greying hair was receding at the temples and he addressed his dish with a kind of religious intensity. Then he turned to Trudi as she said something, his expression of polite enquiry scarcely masking something else lurking in his eyes, a purple sheen of anger compounded with arrogance. Lara watched him while a team of waitresses moved adroitly among the tables, carefully removing the dishes and replacing knives and forks. She recalled the saga: marriage break-up was often difficult and painful, divorce messy and divisive, but this man, it seemed, had reneged on every promise he had made his wife. At first he had visited the children and supported them financially, but since he had shacked up with another woman this support had dried up. It was bearing all the responsibilities unaided together with the pressures of her work that had precipitated Naomi's nervous breakdown. Lara's eyes moved anxiously to her, sitting between John and the best man. She saw with admiration that despite her pallor she was smiling.

A waiter indicated that her table should go to the buffet and she followed the other guests. One of Bron's brothers saw Lara looking at him and smiled. He came over and joined her in the queue.

``You're Lara Streete, aren't you?'' he asked.

``Yes,'' she replied, ``and you're Toby, Bron's brother.''

``How do you know?'' he asked.

``Oh, I just put two and two together.''

``You're supposed to teach dancing – not maths.''

``Quite right – What are you doing now?''

``Oh, off to university to run up an overdraft and become an unemployable graduate,'' he said cheerfully.

``How's your mother?'' she asked.

``Oh, sick as a parrot all morning. We thought we'd have to bring her here on a stretcher.''

``She's looking fine.''

``Yes, extraordinary, isn't it? You know she had to ask Dad to come to this shindig – the old bat having forbidden it.''

``The old bat?''

``The new wife – he's married her now.''

``Oh, did she indeed! But your mum still wanted him here?''

``Well, Bron and Imo wanted it, I suppose.''

``Is she better?''

``Still wobbly,'' he said, making little flapping movements with his hands. ``We all are, actually. She's threatened to either sink her teeth into his neck or slide a stiletto between his ribs.''

``It sounds as though it's the new wife that deserves that treatment.''

``Exactly; pathetic, isn't it? But it doesn't stop it hurting.''

``Has he ever explained it to you?'' she asked.

``No; well, not properly. We've only ever got platitudes, half-hearted assurances of good will. Trouble is, that doesn't pay the rent or buy the food.''

``Have you got a grant?''

``Well, most of one, but it's still based on Mum's salary from last year, before she was ill and had to give up work.''

``Mm; stupid, isn't it? But even a full grant doesn't actually give you enough to live on.''

``Don't I know it! James – that's my brother – has already done a year living on rice.''

He heaped his plate with several spoonfuls of coleslaw. ``Talk to you later then,'' he said as they started back to their separate tables.

``I look forward to it. And tell your mother she's looking marvellous.''

``I will, thanks.'' He grinned, and she noticed an incongruous child-like dimple in his cheek.

While chatting to Trudi's Aunt Jane, who was telling her of her visit to Australia, she found her mind wandering to the Grade Three exam candidates, who had less than three weeks in which to learn `The Highland Fling'. Like Imo they had all worked so hard. `They are doing the best they can,' Lara thought; `that's all I can ask them to do.'

The wedding cake was cut, the speeches delivered, the champagne raised aloft and the toasts given. Guests moved between tables, chattering, gathering, re-gathering – another dance, another ritual.

When the master of ceremonies announced that the bride and groom were going to take the floor to start the dancing she watched Imo with pride. She still had incredible grace. Trudi moved onto the floor with John and Mina with her husband. And then, with a shudder of disbelief, Lara saw that Bron's father was approaching her – was asking her to take the floor with him.

``Let's get the three best dancers in action then, shall we?'' he said, ingratiating himself with a smile. And she saw, disturbingly, an older version of the same incongruous dimple she had seen in his son's face.

What should she say? What excuse could she make? – that they had not been introduced? But did his treatment of his wife make it right for her to seem to snub him on this day when all was supposed to be smiles?

Seeing what he took to be modest confusion, he began to pile on the flattery. ``The bride's mother has been telling me all about you, Miss Streete – all about your prestigious dance academy . . .''

(`And she told me all about you!' Lara thought.)

``Not ballroom dancing, though,'' she excused herself; then, hoping that didn't sound too deprecating, added ``It's just not my *métier*.''

``I'll believe that when I see it,'' he rejoined. And, despite herself, she found herself guided onto the floor with the other couples.

``You don't approve of it?'' he asked, sensing her reluctance.

``No, I admire it – '' she could not admit to him that she loathed it – ``but I'm no good at it. I become wilful and find I'm leading.''

``Well, I shall have to be the perfect partner, then,'' suiting the action to the words.

It was not easy for Lara to admit to herself that he was a really expert dancer. And he seemed to make his lead really easy for her to follow, so that when she found herself quick-stepping with him in and out of the more plebeian couples it seemed to be all her doing. He even seemed to anticipate the help she would need through steps that did not come naturally to her.

``Now the reverse whisk . . .'' he said.

It was something she had never mastered and hardly dared attempt, yet now it was no soon attempted than achieved – whilst the clarinettist wove posies of quavers in coronets round their ears and ever more feet slid across the pulsating floor.

As they swept past Trudi and John, Trudi hissed at Lara ``Come to show us up?''

Lara laughed, but a sudden doubt entered her head. She looked around for Naomi, and saw her sitting looking thoughtfully at her wine glass, listening to her sister. In an

instant the spell – the bond binding dancing partners – was
broken; she almost stumbled. For the first time she sensed
something in his dancing that was calculatedly, insidiously
malign, which the need to respond to the sheer virtuosity of
it had obscured till now. Somehow she stood up till the end
of the dance. Then, thanking him, she said ``Will you promise
me something''

He bowed low: ``Mademoiselle has only to ask –''

``Will you ask you wife for the next dance – your ex-wife
I mean?''

``Ex is right,'' he muttered darkly. ``Don't you think she's
led me enough of a dance as it is?''

``But today of all days – for Bron and Imo's sake?''

He did not meet her eye, but shook his head with a bitter
laugh. ``If I keep one promise I break another. Besides – ''

``Yes?''

``I'm bound over to keep the peace. If I should dance with
Naomi we would quarrel.''

``But how can you be sure if . . .''

As the clapping died, they found themselves surrounded
by other dancers and spectators innocently congratulating
them on their performance, which allowed him to elude her
questioning by a show of disclaiming any credit for himself,
in favour of his partner.

He left her feeling used, flaunted, a vehicle for his
undying, persistent pride. And she felt again the power of
dance as an organ for the expression of all emotion, not only
of joy and hope and reconciliation but also of bitter anger,
vengeance and smouldering resentment.

As the dancing resumed the floor became more crowded.
The best man's girl friend led Bron's grandfather into the fray.
She burbled to Bron ``I've collared the best guest at the
wedding. I only wish I had a bag to take him home in,'' and

she winked broadly at her partner, whose face creased with pleasure.

Trudi came up to the table where Lara was hearing Aunt Jane's Australian trip for the third time. ``John says, can he get you another drink?''

``Oh, lovely. Yes, white wine please,'' she answered.

``I think Naomi is going,'' Trudi said, as she sat down. ``Oh, do you know I'm getting arthritis in my toe joints. I can't wear high heels like I used to.'' She eased a foot out of a shoe. ``Did you talk to her, Lara?''

``Yes, I did,'' Lara revealed, ``but I couldn't really believe what you said – all she'd been through – is going through.

``What did you talk about?''

``She just said how lovely Imo was, how lucky Bron was, what a supportive family you were and how wonderfully you'd organised it all.''

``Well, of course, that's true,'' said Trudi, and they laughed at her own immodesty.

The clarinettist was now playing soprano sax and `My Funny Valentine' was being improvised upon with great adroitness.

``They're a jolly good band,'' Lara acknowledged.

``Bron's choice,'' said Trudi. ``He's been marvellous – like a rock – and Naomi said he was the shyest of all her children. Who'd have believed it?''

``Ah, the love of a good woman – '' Lara began. ``Has the father gone?'' she went on.

``Oh yes, he sneaked away without a word soon after you took the floor with him.''

``Really!''

``Under orders, I expect.''

``You know, Trudi, the thing that I find so hard to take is that an accomplished dancer can be such a worm when it comes to real life.''

``Ballroom!'' Trudi corrected her. ``There's ballroom dancing for you! We neither of us ever much cared for it, remember?'' And they both laughed again.

``But the boys are so well behaved,'' Lara protested.

``Well, they've been with Naomi for the last eight years,'' Trudi said, ``but I gather he had been a good father, despite everything – up till then.''

``You can't just lose that ability,'' said Lara.

``You can lose the will to exercise it,'' said Trudi, ``or the guts to make the choice,'' – thinking, Lara realised with a flash, of the choice Trudi herself had made between her dance career and domesticity.

``It's always these occasions with Relatives,'' Lara said. ``Relatives with a capital R. It's so difficult marrying our idealised images of them with what they really are.''

``Mmm,'' said Trudi, ``and they can't be other than the people they are. Bron's father did come, and I suppose that was the most he could do. That and no more.''

``But he did,'' said Lara; ``he swirled me off my feet under Naomi's nose, the show-off.'' To John, arriving with more white wine just then, she added ``Tell her to relax now. It's been a wonderful, wonderful day. Well done, both of you.'' And, when he had refilled it, she lifted her glass to them both.

Trudi looked up. ``Oh, I think Aunty Elsie is going; I must say goodbye.''

She got up from the table and John followed in her footsteps; the clouds of music drifted after them, and then closed behind them like doors.

Lara looked round at the remaining guests. The best man and his girl friend were locked in each other's arms, rotating slowly to the music. Bron's great-grandfather and Naomi's sister and her husband and children were smiling goodbye.

Mina and Aunty Jane had arms round each other's shoulders; Lara supposed Mina was hearing yet more of the Antipodean saga. One of Trudi's nephews, bow-tie askew, shirt hanging out of his trousers, was leaning back and yawning. A group of men by the bar were exchanging jokes and laughing. Trudi was guiding Aunty Elsie to the door whilst nodding sagely at her.

Miss Streete cast her eye over them all, thinking `We delegate roles for each other but can only play successfully what we are. Marriage comes when we try to bring together, hold together, one in either hand, these two disparate entities: one, what we are seen to be by other people and the other, what we know ourselves to be. We only have a chance of effecting this integration if we are honest. If we sacrifice the honesty, the effort is useless.

`I hope I manage to play the role of teacher and friend,' Lara thought. `For better or for worse, I never had the opportunity of being a wife or a parent. Perhaps wedded bliss is a metaphor implying any such effort is a blessed state. I can only see that some people are not yet contemplating any such union, and for them no clouds of confetti and rice are beating round their heads like mayflies on a summer's eve. Just as dancers fight their recalcitrant bodies to bring their shapes and movements into an idealised form and the gruelling round of *barre* work and exercises is their marriage contract, so humanity chooses to enter another contract. Not everyone wants the effort involved. And who can blame them?' Lara laughed, remembering cramp, bleeding toes, legs that creaked with any movement, limbs that felt leaden in bed at dawn.

`Who'd be married, or even engaged? – engagement being a word that acknowledges a fight is about to begin. `A wedding, I suppose, is that most difficult of unions – the marriage between the role and the reality.'

The Other Rite of Spring

THE night had already spread its shadows deep inside the hall. Some of the fluorescent lights were on the blink; a couple winked uncertainly whilst the motor of another buzzed to itself, providing an irritating background tone against which the music from the tape recorder sounded tinny and constrained.

Lara came over from her chair to the seat where Jenny sat. Jenny noticed how her skin looked pale and the indigo shadows under her eyes sunk them deeper into their sockets, and the image of the old lady that she would some day become looked out of her face.

``Thinking out those last few bars and making the steps is increasingly like squeezing blood from a stone,'' confided Lara.

``More coffee?'' Jenny asked.

``Definitely,'' she smiled. ``Black and very strong,'' she added.

Jenny got up from the table. ``I expect Clara'll want one,'' she said. ``I'll ask her, although I expect she'd prefer tea.''

Lara returned to the group of waiting girls, who having taken advantage of her lack of attention, were sitting on the floor in a rough kind of circle, chatting and laughing. One of them pulled on a large sweat shirt and another wrapped a cardigan round her shoulders and tied the sleeves in a loose knot on her chest.

``Come on, now,'' Lara called, desperately hoping that her brisk tone would imbue them and her with new life and energy.

``Let's go from the oboe solo; Tracy, Suzanne, that's your bit: step, step, *glissade*, *posé*, *fondue*, *arabesque* . . . '' She went over the steps herself and as she said them, marked them quickly for the girls. They pulled themselves to their feet, watching her, outlining the steps with their eyes and making vague hand movements. She saw the gleam of intelligence in their glances and they dispersed, scattered and took up their positions. She walked over to the tape recorder, and felt her legs aching as she crouched down to see the number counter so as to find the right place on the tape.

The music started and Miss Pruett turned her knitting in her lap and started upon another row.

Jenny came in with a tray. Lara took her mug absent-mindedly, watching the dancing, watching her creation, watching the shapes and patterns unfold and wondering whether it was adequately conveying the nuances of feeling and waves of passion she heard in the music; knowing all the time that she was asking more of the children than they knew how to convey, more in terms of worldly experience and more in terms of balletic technique. She sighed. And yet, always, they astonished her, and she felt overwhelmed with gratitude to them.

She watched every step. Suddenly Jane moved, on cue, into a series of *demi-contretemps*.

``No! No!'' she said. Jane stopped and looked at her, blushing slightly. She pressed the pause button on the tape recorder. The other children stopped. The darkness seemed to crowd into the room.

``You can't stick your leg out like that when you do a *demi-contretemps*,'' she complained. ``It's almost a fourth you've got there. It must be *derrière*. Right behind.'' She pushed Jane's leg firmly behind her as the girl put it into the air.

``It's a low *arabesque* line,'' Lara continued. ``Come on, place it properly for me.''

Jane moved her leg again into place.

Lara regarded it critically. ``Push the hip down,'' she said. ``Right; good, that's right,'' and she took a few steps back, holding Jane's extended arm with her hand and regarding her line.``What does it feel like?'' she asked.

``It hurts,'' said Jane, somewhat petulantly.

``Right,'' she said, ``Good! You know when it hurts that it's right.''

The rest of the girls laughed and Jane managed a small smile. They had all heard this so many times before that the appalling honesty of Lara's statement no longer surprised them. And yet every time she said it she knew she was feeding them some dreadful truth, the mystery of which, the morality of which, she did not want to consider. She joined in the laughter to dispel some of the horror of it.

``So; right,'' she said, ``when you end the *contretemps*, you must be there;'' and she indicated with a nod of her head the final position. ``See it more as a *chassé passé* and a *posé, temps levé*, yes, yes; drive into the ground, more *plié*, more *plié*, and then lift.''

She showed them what she meant, talking them through it. ``Jump and leave the leg behind, but always with the feel of urging the head and shoulder forward; lead out of the *sauté* with the shoulder.''

Jane and the rest of the girls followed her.

``Can I have some music, Miss Pruett?'' she called. Clara put her knitting into her lap and, watching the steps, picked up the rhythm and joined them with notes on the piano.

``On, on,'' said Miss Streete, much happier now with the

step; ``let's pick it up where we left off.''

She glanced at the clock nervously, very aware of the passing of time. There was half an hour left and still so much music unchoreographed. The performance was four weeks away and strictly speaking that meant only four more sessions with this particular group of girls, although she knew she could probably call them for another two rehearsals.

``Thanks, Miss Pruett,'' she called and released the pause button on the tape recorder.

The dancing continued and then suddenly ceased. This was as far as they had got. The children faltered and then stopped. Lara looked at them in dismay. She felt herself shuddering and inwardly quaking with fear. She listened to the music ploughing on implacably, delineating tracts of uncharted ocean waiting to be sailed, explored and made explicable. Two things were happening simultaneously within her. One was a rising panic at the blankness of her mind, the other was a straining to empty her mind of everything but the music. She needed to give herself time to trust in her innate ability to hear it, absorb it and then transmute it into movement. There was always the surge of anxiety eating away at the edges of her creativity, threatening to disperse it in an intangible puff of vapour. She listened and started to see it. She ran over and stopped the tape recorder and ran back to the dancers.

``Right,'' she said, ``mark this,'' and quickly she outlined the movements she wanted, grouping and regrouping the dancers with the steps and poses that the music demanded. She heard it in her head and as it unwound she also unwound its physical equivalent. Then again she heard the notes pouring out relentlessly and she had no more steps with which to talk about it. She stopped. Looked up at Jenny, defeated. ``Oh it's hopeless,'' she muttered, ``that's as far as I can go.''

The girls looked at her.

``All right,'' she said to them, ``Let's go from the very beginning.''

She moved back to the tape recorder and rewound the whole tape. The reel rattled slightly and the twilight tones in the hall fluttered behind her as the children chatted, conferred and took up their starting positions.

``Why on earth do we do this?'' she asked Jenny, not for the first time, later on, as they were tidying up. They were bringing the washed-up coffee cups from the kitchen and putting them in the cupboard, together with a forgotten pair of ballet shoes, the register, the tapes and Clara Pruett's music.

``There're only four weeks left and great chunks of it aren't even choreographed, let alone rehearsed.''

She threw some papers and her dancing shoes into her bag. Jenny scrabbled under the table for a carrier bag.

``We'll never be ready,'' Miss Streete said. ``I never get the same group of dragonflies together on a Saturday – I don't suppose one child has been all the way through the whole dance.''

``Yes, we will,'' said Jenny.

``We will what?''

``Be ready.''

Miss Streete was silent. The buzzing of the light was beginning to get to her and increase her agitation.

``We always are,'' said Jenny quietly.

``But there's always a first time, isn't there – the one where it all falls apart?''

``It won't,'' said Jenny. ``Now, can you spare five minutes to look at Caroline's head dress? I'm not sure this is what you wanted.''

Lara swung herself up onto the table, wincing at the twinges in her thigh muscles.

Jenny produced a confection of net and tinsel from the bag.

``Oh, it's lovely,'' Lara said, caught again by Jenny's remarkable ability to twist and turn fabrics into a fairy-like creation. ``You are clever,'' she added.

``But is it what you want?''

``Oh yes,'' she said. ``We must see it on her and she must try moving in it. But that's perfect.''

She sighed.

She had to face going home in isolation from her raw materials, as it were, and ponder over her dance. She knew from experience what difficulties were made by the regular impounding of the stuff of her craft. She couldn't reach for a piece of paper and scribble down a felicitous phrase or grab a palette and mix exactly the colour she knew she needed for a part of the canvas. All was regulated by the availability of the dancers. And they weren't a regular troupe, a band of professionals chosen by her, trained to the very pitch of their abilities, but her pupils, young children quite a few of whom were reluctant scholars anyway. Yet every child would have a part; all would be given opportunities to dance in groups or on their own. It was as a handicapped artist, she put it to herself, that she had to make her creations. It was like being asked to paint with only two of the primary colours or write a symphony excluding one whole section of the orchestra. Restraints, she knew, often drew from her some of her more inventive ideas, but there was a limit to their usefulness. Entrances and exits had to be decided with a view to following numbers, allowing certain children time for quick changes of costumes. The costumes themselves had often to be borrowed and re-used; she was more than familiar with the constraint of keeping costs down. Even though Jenny wrought miracles with old net curtains, old bridesmaids' dresses and very often her own and Lara's and Annabel's clothes, there were always some mothers who grumbled at the price. Jenny often said those parents thought things like zip fasteners, elastic and cotton grew on trees or appeared out of thin air.

She was also terrified of some catastrophe that could wreck a production: an epidemic of German measles, a fractured ankle, sometimes just a broken commitment would mean a headaching rejigging of the cast and a hasty reorganisation of costumes.

``Anyway,'' said Lara, ``I'll take the tape home and see if I can't dredge up some ideas before next week. If all else fails I'll look at some of my ballet video tapes and swipe some ideas from them. – Which the children won't be able to do,'' she added, then said ``I do wish they'd do something about that light. Fluorescent lights don't have a beneficial effect on me at the best of times, I'm sure they give me headaches; that buzzing does nothing for my peace of mind.''

``I'm seeing old Conway about the extra hours we want the hall,'' said Jenny carefully storing away the head-dress. ``I'll have a word with him about it. Oh, and what about this?'' and she dived deeper in the bag and produced a swatch of cotton material.

``A bit minimalist, isn't it?'' Lara said, laughing. ``What is it?''

``It's a piece of cotton I dyed, possibly for Liam's shirt. Is that the colour you want?''

Lara considered.

``Rather a lemony yellow, isn't it?'' she said. ``I think it ought to be more creamy.''

``Mmm,'' said Jenny looking at it, holding it over her fingers.

``But too creamy looks white under the lights. I'm not sure

I can get anything in between.''

Lara was always nervous of being discouraging. She knew Jenny deliberated and fretted over the rightness of the costumes as she did over the steps. She didn't want to hurt her, but Jenny always placed her firmly in authority and Lara knew that if she got it wrong it would be her own fault. She found it was best to be positive rather than to prevaricate.

``Well, we'll see it with the rest of his costume, but I think it'll kill the colour of his shorts.''

``Mm.''

``Anything else?''

``No.''

``How's it going?''

``Oh, all right,'' Jenny said in her usual optimistic way.

``Do you need any money or anything?'' Lara asked.

``Umm. No, not yet. I may need some on Saturday.''

``I'll give you a cheque,'' said Lara. ``I'll give you a cheque now. I don't think you should be out of pocket.''

``Oh, all right then,'' said Jenny and producing a sheaf of bills and an old exercise book started totting up a column of figures.

``Can you still see if I turn that wretched buzzing light off?'' Lara asked.

``Yes, I expect so.''

They conferred over the figures and Lara gave her the cheque.

``I expect I'll find Conway in the church tonight,'' Jenny said, ``so I'll go that way.''

``OK. I'm off. I'll see you Saturday, but ring if there're any problems in the meanwhile,'' Lara said, smiling.

She gathered up her battered leather handbag, her dancing bag and the tape recorder and started out of the door. Jenny ran to open it for her.

``Can you manage?'' she asked.

``Yes,'' Lara laughed, ``eventually I always manage.''

Jenny watched her stagger to her car. She saw the face gaunt and monochromatic in the sodium glare from the street lighting. She watched with pity as she would a dying man, but knowing that if she applied bandages to his wounds he would pluck them off and impatiently throw them into the gutter, where his seeping blood would follow, slowly draining out of him.

There was no stemming obsession.

It was six months ago or thereabouts, she recalled, certainly back in the summer, that Miss Streete and she had booked seats at the Opera House to see a visiting ballet company and some of their more publicly acclaimed guest stars. It had been a heat-ridden day and the ballet company were in indifferent form, the house unbearably stuffy. The eye was constantly distracted from the illuminated handkerchief that was the stage by the twinkling of a myriad fans and programmes, all fluttering vainly in an effort to create a draught to keep the balletomanes cool. Miss Streete had given Jenny a conspiratorial nudge and whispered ``I've booked the theatre.''

``Oh,'' Jenny had said in mock solemnity, ``I thought you were never doing another show.''

Lara did at least look sheepish. At the end of every production she always announced that this was her last.

In the interval, when they were sipping wine together in the bar of the ampitheatre, Lara spread an envelope on the bar, smoothing out the creases, revealing some writing. She took a sip of her wine and said ``Come on Jenny, help me shuffle these names around; if I don't cast it I'll never be able to start.''

Jenny looked. She couldn't always make out Lara's writing.

``I'm not sure quite how many acts to have, and I think I'll need someone who is good at mime. Since Becky left there hasn't really been anyone in the school to replace her and what do you think if I include . . . ''

Jenny looked at her and considered that if this were divine discontent it certainly did not have any divine conviction about it, and then wondered which was the more dangerous commodity, the more disturbing madness. She found her eyes straying to the cheesecake and she gazed at it with guilty longing.

``The trouble is,'' she said to Lara, ``that I try to curb my appetite and stay slim. When I do eat something, after holding out for a couple of hours I positively feel it rushing to all the fat parts to plump them up.''

``Have a slice?'' Lara asked impishly.

``Why not?'' said Jenny, sighing. ``One indulgence being every bit as bad as another – '' and she looked at the piece of paper again.

``Indulgence?'' said Lara innocently.

``Something like that,'' said Jenny, and then, ``who have you in mind as the principals?''

And that was how it had started, again.

She stowed her own things in her car and then, seeing the lights in the main body of the church, moved towards the door. She heard muffled strains of music – the organist practising for a forthcoming wedding, she supposed. She entered the church, following the sound; on attaining the main aisle she was swamped by the full burst of music. Hearing the deep notes thunder from the organ, Jenny was reminded of the gaping wound of an empty stage, yawning and yearning under the tender proscenium. There was something piteous and yet glorious about it. Hearing the bass notes, she coupled that aching void with human aspiration and human despair. Somewhere, she thought, she had got the church and the theatre confused. They both inspired feelings of awe and a sense of the sublime. Had she been a medieval woman she might have embraced religion, become a nun, or laboured to become a divine like Julian of Norwich. As it was, she had allowed herself to become enslaved to the theatre. She had aided and abetted Lara Streete whenever she had embarked upon a production with a devotion which Lara herself had denounced as insane. At which Jenny laughed, agreed and knowingly connived.

In a life that had been joyless in many respects, these ventures were a welcome distraction. She could put a lot of energy into an activity that would have a tangible, if brief life. Lara placed all the ingredients in the magic box, but she was responsible for painting the arcane symbols on that box, giving it the icons of mythology, so that as each child stumbled into the bewildering sea of light on the stage they shone as clearly as the stars in the night sky, the mysterious sign-holders of an ancient ritual.

She never doubted that it would work; it always had done, on every occasion, at every performance. She never probed the mysteries, only offered herself to their manifestation. She never doubted the thread of life, spanning the centuries, that allowed ancestors their say, nor that the cells of this generation of dancers held encoded signals culled from every century of man's history. For within the tissue of every man living today there was held captured, like a fly in amber, the pattern and form of man's past. And the past was so big and so immense, that contemporary actions were trifling activities of no more moment than the beat of a moth's wing. But each cell of the *soma* had memories of the pounding of drums, the beating of hoofs and the cry of fear from the wild. So it wasn't to be wondered at that one throbbed at the sight of the cow parsley unfurling, the first snowflake falling or the smell of rain in the grey-green distance; for the older and more ancient the memories, the more body space they must occupy. Our tissues, too, know more of paganism than of ordered religion, the ritual processional that Nature taught us still holds the heart in thrall, still makes the soul leap at the sight of sunrise, rather than at the roar of a jet engine. Noble philosophies and humanitarian tracts occupy such a small fraction of our bodily selves, whereas gesture and movement drawn from deep stirrings in the earth cut like knives across the surface of our consciousness.

The dance needs no explanation. Its measure, which can be idle chatter or heart-breaking absolutes, communicates deeply, wordlessly, from being to being.

And really there was little difference she thought, now, between theatre and stage, religion and temple. They were essentially in the same line of business: man either crouched in god like a Delphic oracle, or god crouched in man like Christ. They both required an audience, they both operated through a priesthood. Involvement in either was called a vocation. She could not deny hers, and doubted that Lara could. To do so would be simply to deny their natures.

Miss Streete stood on the darkened stage, her back against the curtains – the front tabs – and glanced down at her watch. It was spot on half past. She looked into the wings. They were shrouded in darkness, like graves awaiting her summons to issue forth their ghosts. She glanced up at the lighting box and saw the pale ghost-faces of the crew watching her. From the other side of the curtains she could hear the excited murmur of the voices of the audience, the rustling and bustling sound that eager anticipation produced. There was the glow of the tab warmers, softening the red shades of the velvet curtains and she could see, through the margin at the top, the strip of yellow that indicated that the house lights were still on.

``They're all waiting for me,'' she thought, neither nervous nor afraid, but thrilled and suddenly imbued with an overwhelming stream of power in her body.

``I can keep them all waiting if I want. The children in their dressing-rooms, the backstage helpers, the audience, the crew, the front-of-house staff, the bar tenders and the programme sellers. They are all waiting for me to say go.''

She stopped hearing the burbling, wave-breaking sound of the audience. She looked at the stage. Here on this little area of the mighty planet Earth, because of the focusing of human attention, because of the magic of a dramatic device called the proscenium, the strange displacing activity called theatre was about the happen. She looked upstage, left, to the wings.

``Jenny,'' she said softly.

Jenny's white face appeared.

``Ready?'' she asked.

``Yes, we're ready,'' came the reply.

``Liam,'' she called.

He emerged from under Jenny's arm, holding a skipping rope and a ball.

``Right,'' she said, ``get ready – find the place.''

He did.

``OK?'' Her voice was light and suddenly unshackled.

She looked at him. He was perfect.

She looked up at the lighting box.``Mark?''

``Yes,'' came a voice.

``Ready?''

``Yup.''

``OK. House lights down. Start the music.''

She stayed in position. She heard the audience respond to the dimming of the lights. A tangible silence surged at her from behind the curtain, and into it the music seeped; persuasive, seductive. There was a last cough and a rustle from the auditorium.

She listened carefully to the music, gave Liam a wink, then looked up again at the crew.

``OK. Front tabs; bring up the stage lights; follow-spot when you see Kathy.''

And like a ghost she vanished into the wings as the curtains parted.

Jenny had a line of butterflies waiting for their entrance. She sidled up to her.

``Any problems?''

``I think Tracy's ribbon is going to need a stitch, but she's in character shoes in the first act; I can put in a quick stitch in the interval,'' Jenny whispered.

She nodded and moved into the main dressing-room.

Two sea nymphs were embellishing their eye make-up with blue glitter. They ignored her. The dressing-room was quiet. In a corner a moth sat on a pile of props reading a book with its walkman playing. She turned and looked into the mirror with its garland of lights.

``Who am I?'' she thought, looking at her face, her daunted, haunted eyes, the rings under them and the wrinkles at the edges.

``What right have I to style myself puppet master?''

A shuffling noise from outside and a procession of blue gauze wings caught her attention. The butterflies were filing quietly onto the stage. She moved quickly into the wings again.

Before her eyes the story unfolded. Mentally she made every movement, even if she couldn't properly hear the music or see the dancing; it unwound in her head like the tape spool from which it was playing.

She lay the lattice of what was actually happening, when she glimpsed it, across the blue-print in her mind of what should be happening; cross referring all the time, willing the two images to come together, to be one. Sometimes they did and she was content, sometimes they didn't; an arm movement was late or a circle misplaced in its position on the floor, and she strained to achieve the coupling by her will alone.

And all the time the energy flowed out of her like blood into the libation bowls.

In the last interval she changed from trousers and T-shirt into a smart cocktail dress, `the little black number', as she jokingly called it, with which she would take her bow. She fled to the back of the theatre and watched the finale, and then the beginning of the bows being taken, until she knew she could leave it no longer and she ran down and scampered round back stage to wait in the wings for her bow.

At this point she considered, stopped and took a slight pause for judgement. And it came as no surprise to find that the progeny of six months' solid work was suddenly no longer hers. And this happened every time; her creation slipped effortlessly from her grasp and became something else with its own separate life and identity. It had come through her, certainly; she remembered the pain and the struggle, but she felt no more than the means of giving it existence. It had come from the ether and been redelivered thither.

And suddenly recognizing her cue she walked onto the stage, temporarily blinded by the lights, staring into the void of the auditorium, which throbbed with warmth of feeling and the vibrant rhythm of applause. She smiled and smiled and she bowed and the clapping increased. And she felt more and more, the longer she stood there, that something precious and important had fled away from her.

The smallest children in the school came on with flowers for her and the separation became overwhelming, until surrounded by colour, bathed in the warm rosy stage lights, she felt herself the most lonely person in the universe, with a coldness inside her like the ice of the purest diamond.

The curtains finally closed and the stage darkened and then re-lit with the working lights. Beyond the tabs the house lights came up. The children scattered to their dressing-rooms and the stage crew were laughing quietly as they moved along one of the catwalks that ran round the stage. From the auditorium she overheard the warm contented murmuring of a congratulated and congratulating audience, chatting to their exhausted and excited offspring.

She grasped her flowers, feeling that even these did not belong to her. The coldness made her flesh crawl and she felt the hairs stand up on her arms. A call of goodbye and congratulations came from a group in the wings. She couldn't hear it properly, so fast was the world being closed out. But she smiled and acknowledged the thanks.

Jenny moved from the wings. A strand of damp hair fell across her eyes, and over her arm she had four head-dresses draped. A string of safety pins fell from her collar. She looked at Lara's defeated face.

``There's a large you-know-what waiting for you in the dressing-room,'' she said.

``You'll join me?'' Lara asked. What could they do but comfort each other in their mutual loss?

``I don't need much persuading,'' Jenny said.

Miss Streete forced a smile to her lips.

``Come on now,'' said Jenny. ``You know what you always say; if it hurts it's got to be right.''

Autumn

HOW grey the skies, how dark the day. Already the winds of winter were scampering across the garden and insinuating the arthritic fingers of frost into the soft flesh of the flowers. Miss Streete struggled from her bed and moved softly across the carpet to her mirror. She looked at a face slightly but perceptibly sagging at the corners. She wondered for how many more mornings she could summon up her blood and courage and creep through the fallen cloud to her dancing school. The red leaves from the Virginia Creeper lay like bloodied scabs on the pavement.

Miss Pruett was overwhelming the pupils' aching limbs with a Chopin *ballade* when Karina Ballard came into the hall with her daughter Agnes. Miss Streete pushed her legs down into the full *plié* and met Karina's eyes. She noticed the cheerful smile round the painted lips and the slight cluster of mauve shadows that were wrinkles on her forehead. She let her glance move along the dishevelled rows of abandoned chairs round the edge of the hall and saw Karina exchange some words with Jenny and then slip into one.

Annabel, having brought Miss Streete her coffee at the end of the *barre* work, hitched her leg-warmers higher up her legs and moved into the pupils' back line. As they started work in the centre, she started doing the same exercises and Miss Streete could see the pupils glancing at her from the sides of their eyes. She appreciated how Annabel was showing them the shapes and presentation of the steps that they needed to see.

She moved behind Clara Pruett's chair and, laughing as she looked at the music over her shoulder, said ``I think I'll get Annabel to do the bounding in the Highland Fling – if I do it this morning I think I'll fracture something.''

Miss Pruett looked first out of the window and then back at Lara. ``I'd be happy to do something that warms me up,'' she countered. ``It seems to get colder and colder. I thought we were supposed to be worried about global warming.''

``I know it's the wrong thing to say ecologically,'' Lara confided, ``but I quite welcome the thought of the weather getting warmer – maybe it's because as I get older my blood is getting thinner.''

Jenny approached the piano. ``Karina is waiting for a word,'' she explained.

``Oh, I know,'' said Miss Streete. ``Annabel,'' she called, ``come and take over.''

``Aye aye, captain,'' said Annabel.

``Oh, goodness,'' said Miss Streete, ``the staff are getting insubordinate.''

She and Jenny moved back down the hall and Lara stopped by Karina Ballard. The heady scent of Gianfranco Ferre hit her, and Karina's earrings swung in the light like Indonesian temple percussion instruments.

``I know I shouldn't intrude,'' Karina said, ``and I know we're seeing *La Fille* together next month, but there's something I thought I should tell you.''

``It's OK,'' said Lara. ``Annabel's doing the rest of the class – is Agnes doing this class as well?''

``If you don't mind,'' Karina said.

``You know I don't.''

``I'll pay the extra –'' Karina started to reach for her purse.

``Oh, don't worry,'' said Lara, and then added ruefully
``This is why I arrive in a new BMW every year.'' Then, in
case it sounded sarcastic, she said ``I do love those earrings,
Karina. They are really glamorous.''

``All designed to cheer,'' Karina nodded. ``But they really
attack my lobes.'' And she slowly removed them. ``I'm more
comfortable without them, actually.''

Lara laughed quietly. ``Like a tree shedding its leaves.''

``Like shedding a husband,'' said Karina tartly.

Lara looked at her questioningly.

``Yes,'' Karina elucidated. ``He's finally shacked up with
Angie and asked for a divorce. I suppose so he can get
married again.''

``What do the children think?''

``Oh, I think they're relieved that things are resolved.''
Karina took a purse from her Gucci handbag and put the
earrings carefully in the front pocket.

``And Agnes?''

``Well, it's about her I've come to see you.''

Lara looked up at Agnes's willowy form dancing at the
back of the class, a head and shoulders taller than her fellow
classmates.

Many of the steps that they were performing under
Annabel's critical eye she was doing on *pointe* and occasionally
Annabel would say ``You can do a double pirouette there,
Agnes – and make that a *pas de bourée à cinq pas* instead of the
échappé sauté fermé.'' And Agnes would adapt the *enchâinement*
to make it more demanding, nodding her head, marking the
steps with hands and feet and occasionally asking Annabel
how to count the movements to the music.

Karina continued. ``You know she did much better in her
A-levels than we anticipated and instead of trying for a poly
next year, she's managed to get into a university this year.''

Lara's eyes widened quickly with delight. ``This year! That's great.''

``Well, I think she decided she'd rather get on with it and I also suspect that she thought a year out might be a waste, especially as she knows I'll charge her rent – if I get any alimony it won't be much.''

``What's she reading?'' Lara asked.

``Engineering! Can you imagine what the papers would make of that? – Actress's daughter designs bridges!''

``Well, I hope she keeps on dancing,'' said Lara. ``*Pas de courru* along the scaffolding or whatever.''

``Bound to galvanise the work force,'' said Karina, ``but anyway, I'm afraid she'll be leaving at the end of the week. She'll have to find a flat and get herself moved up to Manchester.''

``Oh, dear,'' said Lara. ``I was hoping she'd get her Inter, you know.''

``It's a shame, isn't it – but you know how it is.''

Miss Streete knew only too well how it was; the sums and logistics played through her head for the umpteenth time. With Agnes leaving she might have to drop the class altogether. The problem seemed unsurmountable. As her older pupils progressed, the classes they attended became longer; they needed the extra hours to learn larger syllabuses and to build up the stamina they needed for the increasing physical demands the dancing made on their bodies. She was constantly urging these pupils to take more lessons, and because she knew the parents couldn't always afford it she dropped the fees. But longer classes meant higher hall hire charges and higher wages for Clara Pruett or any other of the pianists she employed. Sometimes she used tapes to provide music, but knew these were more often a constraint than an aid and less than satisfactory. The very best of her pupils moved on to professional dance training schools. That left her with pupils who were also struggling with the demands that school work made on their time. Small classes at these levels often meant she was working for nothing but she knew that if she charged what was realistic fee she'd put her classes out of reach of the average pocket. And yet, she so wanted these pupils of hers – those that had worked at their craft so diligently for so many years – to continue to enjoy their dancing and to improve their skills.

As Karina left, Lara plopped down beside Jenny and sighed. ``I'm beginning to feel like Madame Arenskaya in `Belle of the Ballet', an old lady with a failing, tiny dance academy.''

``You betray your age when you confess to reading *Girl*,'' said Jenny. ``Anyway, she had dreadful rings under her eyes. Have a Danish pastry. It will help get rid of them – flesh them out as it were.''

``Yes, and flesh out my waist,'' Lara complained.

``I can't see why you can't join the rest of us,'' Jenny complained, and pushed a plate towards her. ``And here's another coffee – and Karina left her cake so you'll have to eat that, too.''

``You take it for Jarvis,'' Lara said.

``Oh, and Karina said if we're getting tickets to see Sylvie Guillem, to count her in – but you'll be seeing her on the 21st, won't you?''

Annabel came up to say ``I need to know the order of those steps now.'' So Lara stood up, and smoothing down her skirt, moved from the table to the centre of the hall.

``It was as though all that time,'' Karina said, putting a Bloody Mary down on the table in the restaurant, ``I had little Walt Disney puffs of smoke tacked behind me – whirling from one activity to another, hurling laundry about, dashing from one child's lesson to the next, washing up the pans whilst dishing up the dinner . . . Oh, sorry,'' – to the waiter hovering for their order – ``We've been so busy gossiping we haven't even glanced at the menu. Could you come back in a few minutes time?'' And she smiled her ingenuous smile.

Lara noticed the laughter lines around her eyes, and the slender fingers holding a cigarette.

Inevitably the waiter was charmed. ``Certainly madam.'' He gave a mock bow and turned, revealing his long hair tied behind in a pony tail.

``Ah Karina,'' she said, ``you still charm them.''

``Only because I know I'm old enough to be his mother,'' replied Karina, pursing her lips ever so slightly. Dipping into her glass, she drew the lemon slice out with her fingers and popped it, whole, into her mouth. Lara watched, astonished.

``Vitamin C,'' Karina winked. ``Offsets the evil effects of the alcohol,'' she explained.

Around them Joe Allens was getting busy. Karina and Lara had been to the matinée of *La Fille* and then walked down from the Opera House, through the milling throng of Covent Garden. Now the evening clientèle were arriving and more and more people were sitting at the tables with their red and white checkered table cloths.

``I do like this place,'' Karina observed. ``The buzz and the hum of it – I don't know why; I don't know any of the names or faces any more. It just has a zingy feel to it.''

``Rubbish,'' Lara said. ``Whenever I'm here with you there's always someone you bump into.''

``Oh, it's only the antiques that recognise me,'' Karina moaned.

Lara sipping her wine quietly, wondered whether she entirely knew her friend. She scrutinised the menu, frowning at it slightly, while Karina lit another cigarette. She decided what to order. She knew Karina had had a hard time bringing up her two girls largely on her own, and despite a few skirmishes, as she called them, had never really been involved with anyone else. Back in the '60s she had had a couple of extremely good parts in two very well-acclaimed films. Then the tide of fortune had changed and her name disappeared from public view. Lara knew this was a source of disappointment and admired how, even in the smallest rôle she played now, Karina brought a style and a class that often outshone the rest of the cast. But there were fashions in films and plays and, she had to admit, in dance: certain faces, certain shapes of body became the ideal and if you had them you were more likely to be noticed and used, and if not – you were passed over.

When the plates arrived, and with them a clean ash-tray replaced and a carafe of wine, Karina looked covertly at Lara under her lashes and laughed. ``No, no, Lara,'' she said. ``My uncle left me some money and I decided to spend it all on me. I don't think I've actually become a total flesh pot.''

``Oh well, good for you,'' Lara said, and chased a prawn round the edge of her plate.

Karina refilled Lara's wine glass and then her own. ``Maybe I'm talking too soon,'' she said, ``but since Agnes went off to Manchester I have felt quite different. I don't know whether it's empty different or new different or just this-is-a-new-era different.''

``Oh, I know that seasonal feeling,'' said Lara with feeling. ``A series of little events, all in swift succession and then suddenly you realise the whole complexion of things has changed; old faces replaced by new, a new focus and a new centre of attention. You'd think it would be termly or annual – well, at least I do – with the school. Sometimes it is but other times it's not."

``I know it sounds quite potty,'' Karina continued, ``but it's almost as though in shedding the reproductive rôle I'm regaining my sanity.''

``Oh God, are you going through that too?'' Lara asked, nervously wondering, like so many others before her, how bumpy a ride her failing hormones were likely to give her mind and body in the next few years.

``Oh yes, just another of Mother Nature's little gifts to the female race,'' Karina said sourly, sighing heavily and draining her glass. ``But – but part of me feels – at least at the moment, a wonderful relief.''

``Mm – well, certainly money-saving in certain areas,'' concurred Lara.

``I know you haven't had children, Lara – well, physically anyway – but you have had an enormous influence on lots of them – and their development – and I think that counts for a lot. But when they're around you all the time – and they are there for life – they are such a –'' and she searched for words – ``a preoccupation.'' She followed the search for words with a search for her cigarette lighter, and lit another cigarette.

``Pudding?'' she asked her friend.

``No room,'' Lara confessed.

``Me too,'' said Karina.

The waiter arrived, smoothly removing the plates and pouring the remains of the carafe of wine into their two glasses. ``Just some coffee,'' Karina replied to his enquiry.

There was a silence, until she went on ``All a tremendous, diverting preoccupation: all that urge to have a boyfriend, get laid, get shacked up, have children, rush around tending to them. It seems – an untimely diversion.''

Lara laughed. ``But it's the thing every biological thing does,'' she expostulated. ``If it didn't, there'd be no more life, no more nothing.''

``I know. But I remember being a much more rational
being when I was young, when I was about seven, and it's as
though the movement towards adolescence, puberty, just re-
arranged all my priorities, with biology taking precedence.''

``Well, you might have kept your head and decided not to
give in to those urges,'' Lara said; ``and anyway, you've had
your career as well.''

``Yeah, well I don't know. The hormones certainly seemed
to win.''

The coffee arrived and the cups and jug and sugar bowl
were put down in front of them.

``I have flowered, fruited and now –''

``Bits of you drop off,'' said Lara tartly.

Karina laughed but went on ``Now I'm regaining my
rational self.'' And a large gentleman in a grey suit and bow
tie came behind her, put his arms on her shoulders and said
``Karina!''

Karina turned round, recognised him, smiled with delight
and saying ``Charles!'' rose, and they embraced.

Lara gave her a glance saying `I told you so,' which Karina
ignored.

``Busy?'' he asked, and Lara watched them launch into
theatrical talk, initiated by establishing the mutuality of their
affection. This depended quite simply on whether either of
them was in or out of work. If either of them were in a
different position from the other the dynamics altered, but if
they were identical then any amount of chat could be
exchanged, as between equals: confessions about the parts that
got away, the diabolical commercial that paid the school fees,
the voice-over that met the telephone bill, gossip about mutual
friends, activities and recent productions seen.

Miss Streete stirred her coffee. She pondered Karina's

words. A madness, she had said. She too dealt with madness; dancers had whirled themselves into states of frenzy since time immemorial; the corybant, the bacchante, the whirling dervish – all touched by madness, serving different gods and goddesses, acknowledging another self – a divine self – a part of nature. And procreation acknowledged another aspect of Nature: the imperative to reproduce. Was there any difference between the two activities, she wondered. And what of love? `Where is love in all this? Is love only a trigger, a means to an end, or a force, the demi-urge that some call god? – Or a strange inspiration that allows humans to confuse their physical and spiritual destinies?

The waves of sound and chatter rolled around her ears, and Karina turned to her and said ``Oh Charles – this is Lara Streete.''

Charles gave her a slightly perplexed smile and Lara knew from long experience that he was trying to remember whether he should know her face or her name from some production, some field of the performing arts.

``She teaches dancing,'' explained Karina, letting him off the hook and placing her friend firmly off the game-board of theatricality, so that Charles could view her with the benign eye he could cast on a non-competitor.

``Pleased to meet you, Lara,'' he was able to say and mean, in a voice calculated to roll over the stalls like thick honey.

Karina turned back to him and assuring each other of their fondest affection, vowing to keep in touch, they bade each other farewell.

As Karina sat down, the waiter sidled up to them and refilled the coffee cups. She lit another cigarette and, scrabbling in her handbag, produced a tissue which she patted at the edge of her eyes and then at the corners of her mouth.

``He's a dreadful old queen,'' she confided, ``but such a

dear – he'll always escort me, you know, if I need him. I must have known him for twenty years." She laughed, and repeated ``Twenty years – we're getting older, Lara.

``So's everyone.''

As the two friends moved off into the autumnal evening, the sequin-edged darkness that is night in the city enveloped them. Miss Streete, examining herself, wondered whether her friend's outpourings had unpicked and revealed any stray strands of regret. She had known love, had fierce passions, but never a lasting relationship nor children of her own. When Jeremy died something else had gone with him. She had known the madness though, and she knew that she handled the fire and lit the flame and served the gods. And who was to say if there was any difference: if the flame were the same, then surely so were the gods.

She watched her friend being ingested by the entrance to the underground. Karina with all passion spent? She remembered her vivid performance with Charles. Never! A passion different from the exclusive activity of parenthood, she supposed, but Karina's self-proclaimed golden glow of Autumn only affirmed, for Lara, something eternal about nature: the immortal thread that linked all artists from generation to generation.

Her final words had been ``Don't forget to give my love to Agnes – and tell her to keep on dancing.''

Flecked With Gold

SURELY, under all this junk, this ephemera, was the thing she was looking for. Miss Streete, principal of the dancing school, was on her hands and knees, head and torso half ingested by a cupboard. Plastic carrier bags rustled as she pulled them towards her and a tap shoe toppled from the top of one of them and clattered onto the floor beside her. She was sure she had a bag of chiffon scarves and pieces of gauze and net in here somewhere.

Annabel's voice came floating from the other end of the hall. ``Turn out Michaela, get your knee right back – and Gemma, don't sickle your foot.''

Miss Streete heard Miss Pruett start the music for *developpés*, and the slow melody unwound across a murmuring couple of mothers in the corner.

She heard Jenny saying to one of them ``Turn the shoe down here, and that's where the ribbon goes, in that corner, and then when you've sewn them on, bring them to me or Miss Streete and we'll cut them to the right length. Don't forget to put R under the right foot and L under the left.''

``No, Gemma,'' called out Annabel, ``you're turning your toe in. I know you're trying to point it, but look in the mirror; it's the wrong shape. Push the heel forward, relax your toe.''

``Have you found them yet?'' she heard Jenny's voice behind her.

``No,'' she panted, turning round. ``But I seem to have

found several other interesting items.''

``Like what?''

``Well, did you know we have several vests, some socks – all odd, two cross-overs, a copy of *The Enormous Turnip*, one shoe, several combs and an anorak in here?''

``An anorak?'' Jenny queried.

The piano playing stopped.

``Let's try on the other side,'' said Annabel, and the bunch of pink-faced little girls turned and faced her as she marched up to the other end of the hall. ``Gemma,'' she added, ``you stay close to the mirror and watch what your toes are doing.''

``I think all that is lost property from the last show,'' Jenny said, ``but it beats me how anyone can not miss an anorak – nor yet a shoe.''

``We put it all out as lost property afterwards, though, didn't we?'' Lara asked.

``Of course,'' Jenny replied, ``but not everyone remembers, or bothers to look.''

``Do you remember what I did with the scarves?''

``The chiffony ones, d'you mean?''

``Mm.''

``They're there; try the bag with the national skirts.''

Lara plunged into the cupboard again. She emerged triumphant. She sat next to Jenny, who grabbed a handful of national skirts and started scrutinising the fastenings and then shaking them free of their creases.

Lara started counting the pieces of chiffon. ``I wonder how Nicola's getting on,'' she said.

``Huh,'' Lara replied. ``We'll know soon enough.''

``It *is* this morning, isn't it?'' Jenny asked.

``You know it is. Gosh – these could do with an iron.''

``These could do with a stitch or two.''

``We'll just have to have some crumpled spectres this

morning," Lara said, frowning slightly.

Annabel came up quickly and took a gulp of coffee whilst the pupils put their chairs noisily against the walls.

``I keep thinking of Nicola,'' she confessed; ``how do you think she'll do?''

Lara shrugged. ``It's in the lap of the gods,'' she said. ``Take arms and *port de bras* and a bit more *adage* and then I'll take over.'' All morning she, too, had had her mind on Nicola who, even now, was attending her final audition for the Royal Ballet School. It was, she felt, more than a coincidence that Nicola's final audition turned out to be on the same day Lara had got half a dozen tickets for *The Nutcracker*. However, even now, she wondered whether it wasn't going to be somewhat ironic. Should Nicola pass, then it would be a wonderful way to celebrate the day – but if she didn't, if she weren't chosen, then how, she wondered, would the little girl weather the experience? Would she still see it as a treat or would it show her a glimpse of something from which she would now feel excluded? How many of us, Lara mused, watch dancing from that viewpoint anyway – one-time practitioners seeing others have the pain and the glory – performing vicariously? Most of us want to be the doers really, she supposed. And as for suggesting that students became doers and auditioned for any of the schools of vocational training, that too often troubled her. She herself had already implemented a selection process, sorted out the children with the right build, the right anatomy as far as she could see, a sense of rhythm and a natural poise, grace and aptitude for movement. And even on these criteria she knew certain children were excluded who possibly should not be. Even if they were wonderful performers, the large-boned, the too tall, the flat-footed were already eliminated.

``I must iron these before next week,'' she said to Jenny, indicating the scarves.

``I'll do them," said Jenny. ``I think I'll take these national skirts home and give them a going over. D'you want another coffee before you start?"

``Are you making one?" Lara asked.

``I expect Clara would like another cup of tea," Jenny said. ``Oh, shall I pick the Lewises up tonight – before you?"

``I expect that'll be better," Lara decided. ``Don't let me forget to sort it out with them before they go."

``I expect Nicola'll be dead on her feet."

``Not if she's passed; she'll be dancing on air," Lara surmised.

Jenny said nothing.

Miss Streete was not sure of the possible outcome of the audition. The one thing she did know was that lack of parental means should not prevent a child attending the Royal Ballet School. But there were lots and lots of other children at dance schools where dance techniques other than pure ballet were being learned who hadn't got that guarantee – and Lara had seen, time and time again, gifted, hard-working children of less-than-wealthy parents denied the opportunity that went to their richer counterparts. They had the chance of combining their general education with training for the stage. All the rest combined daily schooling with weekly dancing classes – and fortunately for them, teachers all over the country offered lessons of a high standard at an often less than profitable, let alone professional fee. Of course, Nicola could always continue with her lessons with her should she not pass, and settle her sights a little lower. But to begin with, there was nothing wrong with aiming high.

There was a small commotion by the door. Mrs Lewis, looking like a wild butterfly, black curls a-flying, eyes sparkling, came towards Lara, before her, her small serious faced blonde-haired daughter.

``Nicola,'' she said, in her husky voice, ``what have you to tell Miss Streete?''

The hubbub had thrown a handful of pebbles into the calm pool of the dancing classes. Miss Pruett looked up from her knitting and Annabel started moving towards the door. The little pupils turned round and watched wide-eyed. Jenny emerged from the kitchen.

``I got in, Miss Streete,'' Nicola gasped. ``I passed.''

Miss Streete felt her tight facial muscles relax into a delighted smile. Her grey eyes sparkled as she caught the excitement in the little girl. ``That's wonderful, Nicola – well done!'' she exclaimed.

Annabel added, ``Congratulations!''

And from all round the room, various whisperings and shouts and calls and cries added to the confused outpouring of relief and good wishes. Miss Pruett actually left her station and sailed towards the knot of people who had now entered the hall and were congregated in a bubbling mass at one end. Jenny had doubled back on herself and re-entered with a trayful of drinks. Mrs Lewis, her elder daughter Sara, Annabel and Nicola and Lara, all buzzed and hummed whilst garbled snatches of the experience were stitched and re-stitched together and a picture of the morning's activities was patchworked together. Laughing and joking, Nicola stood opposite her mother and Miss Streete, hopping up and down, looking from one and telling the other. The other pupils had huddled into a group of their own and were talking excitedly to one another.

Miss Streete detached herself. ``Now,'' she called, and moved towards the centre of the room, ``*this* show must go on – Nicola, do you want to join in?''

Nicola nodded enthusiastically and Lara looked to her mother who also nodded happily.

``Pop out then and change. – I expect Mrs Lewis would like a cup of tea," she went on to Jenny, and then to Miss Pruett, ``you stay and have yours here because we shall use the tape recorder. – Now – where are they?"

She moved to the table and got the scarves. ``Ah, here they are. Now, come with me, everyone else, and I shall tell you what we're going to dance."

The small group of girls followed her into the centre of the hall. She moved towards the table on which she had set up the tape recorder and looked carefully amongst the tapes for Ravel's `La Valse.'

``Let's just sit and listen to some of this music," she said. ``And I'll tell you that the title of what we are going to dance is called `The Haunted Ballroom'. So as you listen, imagine that."

She gathered the group close enough to hear the music – and far enough away from the distraction of the recuperant Mrs Lewis, confident that Jenny and Annabel would extract all relevant information from that source. The music wove its magic. As it played, she saw Nicola re-enter the room. The other girls turned and watched her. Her mother's eyes were on her, and all the other eyes in the room turned towards her and Lara saw what everyone saw. Something, someone, flecked with gold; someone who had been touched with a particular wand, someone, and they were all giving her this quality, even as she set one foot in front of the another, as she gained ground slowly, carefully but ever more surely, down the length of this simple suburban church hall, someone who has been touched by fame.

Nicola accelerated her step as she gained the group, anxious to be embraced, to be safe and usual again. And yet some knowledge prevented her sitting, as she usually did, close to her friend Gemma. She sat a little bit away, a little bit removed.

Lara sensed the separateness as the little girl drew up her knees and hugged them to herself. She faded the music and explained the story. ``There is a ballet called `The Haunted Ballroom','' she explained. ``You may have seen pictures of it – this is not quite the story, but it's the story I want to use to this music.'' And she continued to explain how the room itself with its ghostly music has the ability to lure a young girl into it to make her dance to death – and how each year the ghosts of all the maidens gather there and then, once another poor girl has danced herself to exhaustion, they are all compelled to re-enact their own deaths. Many were the times she and Jenny had laughed over the lurid story lines that the children acted out when they performed these mimes, as she called them. `Dying in great agony' had become what Jenny called the motto of the school. (``I'm sure it would be better in Latin,'' Lara grumbled.) But she knew well enough and remembered well enough her own childhood emotions. She knew that adults, too, often diminished children, seeing them and their world as twee and sweet. She knew they are nothing of the sort. That particular sentiment is projected by the adults themselves. Children are desperately moved by great issues: love, war, death, cruelty, blood and thunder. It needs a courageous but uninhibited adult to have the nerve to release yet control these forces. Lara knew that although steps and exercises are the vocabulary and the technique, the real stuff came from unleashing the passions – letting the feelings speak.

She played them the ending of the music: she saw their eyes widen and the thrill of the drama tighten their muscles. She could also sense the accompanying *frissons* of self-consciousness; she caught Emma furiously nudging the little girl next to her, desperate to unload some of her rising energy into naughtiness. She knew she wanted that energy in Emma's limbs – not diverted into catching the attention of someone else – and she knew that self-consciousness was horribly catching. She stopped the music abruptly, getting their attention, and explained that they all had to do their own dance – they were not to intrude into someone else's and how unfair that was – and how it needed a lot of concentration. She put on the music again and watched them; noticed how rapt and intense Nicola looked, almost white with intensity.

``Now we start quite easily,'' she said, consciously soothing the nervous. ``You are *all* the ghosts gathering in the ballroom – two straight lines coming from each corner – with these on your heads – '' and she produced the gauzy pieces of material – ``like this.'' And she put a piece of gauze over her face.

``No expressions on your face – like ice,'' she explained, ``and you glide rather than walk,'' and she proceeded to move eerily across the floor. Then she removed the scarf and continued. ``But as you walk, you can feel the cold moonlight in the room, the drifts of cobwebs and the strange frightening shadows – you are – *are* the shadows, *you* are the ghosts.''

The girls took the scarves and put them over their faces, turning to look at each other and smile.

She recaptured their attention. ``Now, off you go – you'' – and she indicated one group, ``start from that corner and you lot'' – and her hand circled the remainder, ``start from that one.''

They ran to their places.

``Wait for the music,'' she called.

They waited, suddenly still and silent.

The music started, the hall was hushed and the slow procession of little shapes moved spectrally down the hall. And then it had happened again – now by the simple expedient of placing a veil over their heads she had created, the pupils had created – how she didn't know – something else: ghosts, spectres, *wilis*, the spirits of the dead. She didn't know how the magic worked, she only knew it did.

When Jenny came to pick her up that evening, she already had Mrs Lewis, Nicola and Sara in the back of the car. They greeted each other excitedly and Jenny said ``Annabel will meet us up there.''

``Oh, fine.'' Lara relaxed.

``And she said Steven said `come round to the stage door afterwards and we can go backstage'.''

``Oh, great!'' She turned half round in her seat and addresses the Lewis's. ``That'll be fun, won't it?''

Mrs Lewis nodded in agreement whilst Nicola's and Sara's eyes shone with excitement.

``Miss Streete,'' Sara said.

``Yes?''

``Mummy says now I'm twelve I can have my ears pierced.''

``Great,'' Lara enthused, recognising the latest tangible puberty rite.

``Nicola won't be able to have hers done, now she's going to the ballet school,'' Sara added with considerable complacency.

Lara laughed and secretly congratulated Sue Lewis on her cunning.

``You don't really want sore ears, do you Nicola?'' Jenny asked.

``No,'' said Lara. ``You'll have sore toes soon enough once you start *pointe* work,'' and she heard Nicola laugh with anticipation.

They plaited their way in and out of the streams of London traffic, bedazzled by lights and the hum of a thousand cars and people. They crossed the coal dark river and saw the ghost of St Pauls rise like a crown of smoke and, amongst the dreary slabs of modern office blocks, the dwarfed bridal cakes of Wren's other city churches.

The sound of the orchestra tuning up in the pit never failed to thrill. It was as though the players were combing out all the discordant tangles from their instruments, ready to introduce harmony into the theatre. Then came the dimming of the house lights and the frightening way a cloak of silence permeated by a few anxious coughs descended on the audience. The intensity of expectancy held itself like a knife to Lara's throat and she felt her stomach tighten. The conductor raised his baton and the first few notes of the overture held her in its grasp . . . and then the curtain slid silently upwards.

It had always been one of Lara's pleasures to take people to the ballet. It was the pleasure of introducing anyone to anything that she enjoyed so that she could see the enjoyment spread. She had on some occasions taken coach parties of pupils, mothers and friends, and on others just small groups of anyone who expressed interest. These trips were not without their hazards and sometimes the thanks and expressions of delight did not always compensate for the pains. She remembered the pampered pupil who ate so much of the chocolate her mother had plied her with that she was sick. She remembered the child she had sat next to who gave her mumps, and she remembered telephoning from a call box an inebriated father who accused her of losing his child, when he had been in a pub at the moment when the returning coach had rumbled into the same pub's car park. That night, like this, had been cold and frosty. Tonight, when they hurried backstage there was already ice forming on the top of the puddles.

``What part did you like best?'' she asked Nicola as

Annabel, Sara, Jenny and Mrs Lewis forged ahead, outside the theatre, urging against the cold.

``Oh, when the snow came down, I think,'' said Nicola. ``I thought that *pas de deux* quite the best part of the ballet.

``More than the *pas de deux* in the last act?''

``Well,'' paused Nicola, obviously finding it hard to choose, ``yes . . . although that was very sumptuous . . . I think I preferred the other music.''

Lara laughed. ``Yes, I like that music too,'' she confessed. ``They used to use it for a scene change – but it's too good not to dance to. I'm glad they've choreographed something to it.''

``I'd like to make up dances,'' Nicola divulged.

``Yes, it's fun – but sometimes horribly hard work.''

``Well, so's dancing.''

``Yes, that too,'' Lara agreed. And paused briefly on another of life's bitter ironies, that choreographers, too, have first to be chosen as dancers and are again subject to the same rigid selection process, both anatomical and physical. Whilst the critics decried the lack of choreographic inventiveness in the country, she recalled small gems she had seen put together in various performances in state schools, dancing festivals and local pantomimes, the creators of which, even if they had had the desire to choreograph, may have had their paths stayed by short Achilles tendons or a lack of money.

The back-stage smell of glue and greasepaint assailed Miss Streete's nostrils as Steven led their little group through the dimly lit corridors towards the stage area. Various people hailed him, called – ``Good-night'' and hurried past them. They passed the open door of a dressing-room and Annabel suddenly called``Sherry!'' and a dark long-lashed girl cried out with delight and then embraced her.

Annabel made some introductions and then the two

friends chatted away enthusiastically. Miss Streete caught Jenny and Mrs Lewis scrutinising the flimsy costumes hung negligently behind the door, and Sara eyeing herself in the lamp-surrounded mirror, over the pile of cotton wool balls, flowers, greeting cards and pots and potions that were on Sherry's make-up table. She saw Nicola looking round her, wide-eyed and very pale. She thought about this strange journey – crossing the mystical bounds between fact and fiction, burrowing backstage into the entrails of the theatre in a desperate bid to find the roots of the mystery, to touch the philosopher's stone. Somewhere in here, in the boundary between gods and men, the magic happened. These were people who were touched with the enchantment; surely they held the key. No wonder they were so scrutinised, so often the object of public curiosity.

Nicola was fingering, ever so lightly, Sherry's diamanté headdress. Wonderingly she said, half to herself, half to Miss Streete, ``It's not real.''

Lara agreed. ``No, it's not real – we just see it as real. I suppose it's what we want to see.'' And put her finger casually, yet accurately, on the surprisingly simple truth of the matter.

Epilogue

MISS Streete folded her black teaching skirt, laid the Greek sandals heel to heel and bound them together with an elastic band and then she rolled the pink ribbons round her soft blocks, looking at the frayed satin. Jenny's news had not quite surprised her because, when she first met David, she had seen there was only what she could describe as a partnership feel to them. Jenny had met him in the autumn following her holiday in Turkey, whilst out walking Jarvis, and had told Lara quite unashamedly that she had joined the local Ramblers Association when she had discovered that David spent most of his weekends with them.

Then, in between making out a formal timetable for the forthcoming exam session and marking the register, she said to Lara ``I think we may be talking wedding bells.''

``Jenny!'' Lara exclaimed, and looked at her with surprise.

Jenny had become quite pink, and she started adding up the times of the session again on her fingers. ``Oh, I can never add up sixties,'' she grumbled, and then looked at Lara meaningfully.

``Jenny! Congratulations!'' Miss Streete said.

``Well,'' said Jenny, ``there won't be any great shenanigans – not at our age.''

``Oh, but there must be,'' Lara complained.

``No, quiet and dignified,'' Jenny said, and then laughed with a sapphire light gleaming in her blue eyes.

The rest of the morning had spun away, various pupils and their parents sharing happily in the news.

Miss Pruett put down her knitting and said to Lara, ``Well, who'd have thought it? She's a dark one that one, isn't she? When will it be?''

``I'm not sure,'' said Lara, ``she hasn't said.''

``Well, at least you don't feel as you do with some of these young things, as you do so often nowadays, that it's not likely to last for more than a couple of months.''

Because it was so close to the children's exams now, Miss Streete was even more exacting with her teaching, scrutinising the prospective candidates' every movement, demanding higher and higher standards of technique. And even as she became more demanding she saw some of the children respond and show her with a heart-stopping gesture some element of pure beauty. She caught her breath at the pain and the pleasure – and noticed an appreciative glimpse of admiration in the eye of one of the mothers.

``Claire's really come on, hasn't she?'' she asked Mrs Wells. ``She ought to get a good mark – she's worked hard enough for it.''

``Oh, and she loves it, Miss Streete,'' Mrs Wells agreed. ``It seems the harder you push her, the harder she tries.''

``Ah, well, you've got to be slightly masochistic if you're going to be a good dancer,'' she agreed.

Mrs Wells added ``And did I hear that Jenny is getting married?''

``Yes,'' said Miss Streete, and looked at Jenny who was squeezing a rather large girl into a rather small national skirt. ``Lovely, isn't it?''

But she hadn't been ready for Jenny's remarks at the end of the morning. Jenny was stacking some chairs away and

Lara replacing music and an unclaimed cross-over in the cupboard.

``Lara,'' Jenny said, ``I think I've told you that David's firm is probably moving to Somerset.'' She paused and turned and looked at her.

``Oh!'' Lara felt herself go cold.

``Well, what I'm saying is – well, if he goes – if he has to go,'' and she stumbled slightly over the words, ``then – um – I'll have to go with him.''

``Of course you will,'' Lara heard herself say. ``Of course you will – um. – Do you know yet when that will be?''

``No,'' Jenny said, and giving her friend the only solace she could think of, added ``but you'll be the first to know.''

And then she was gone and Lara was left packing her bag. At the bottom of it was an old pair of shoes she had worn at her first dancing school – completely battered, unwearable – but she had never been able to bring herself to throw them out. She picked up the register and debated whether to take it home with her or not. She opened it and let her eyes wander down the pages. She flipped idly to the beginning of it and noted ruefully how many more names there were then. The downward trend of numbers seemed unstoppable. She sighed deeply. How many times before had she watched this happen, she wondered, and then seen, like a new spring arriving, the numbers pick up again, her phone ringing with enquiries, new faces – enquiring, shy and eager faces, appearing at the church hall door. But for the moment she was dealing with the situation the only way she knew how – and that was to cut back the number of hours the school would be open, saving at least her outgoings. Fortunately, a small annuity from her great uncle had always allowed her to live, but she still had to eat.

*   *   *

Evening was falling and she shivered slightly as she moved into the living-room to light the fire.

Clara Pruett's phone call came like a thunderbolt.

``Lara, dear – I've been agonising over when to say this – but as you know, I've not been well and although they say I've recovered I've decided to take early retirement. Well, I've been asked to do more hours at the Blakemore Academy – and I really cannot turn down the opportunity of earning a little more.''

And although Miss Pruett was regretful and polite, Miss Streete heard her giving her notice.

When she put the phone down something heavy moved from her stomach to the back of her throat and then caught at her breath and she gave a sob. And was cross with herself. It was all so reasonable; it was just that she herself wasn't.

She gazed at the flames and saw the kaleidoscoping figures of her pupils fluttering and flickering across her vision. She remembered Netta who had preceded Annabel as her assistant, and various older pupils who had taken the beginners, or the `babies' as they were wont to be called: a pageant of people who had passed through her school. Even Annabel, her present assistant, tended to come and go if she got other work. In her experience, she'd known other schools where the assistant teacher had become so popular that she herself had opened a nearby school and poached a lot of her former employer's pupils. This she deemed a dreadful betrayal. She had to admit that part of her felt betrayed by Jenny and Clara Pruett. And then she thought of the countless people like Jenny, mothers whose introduction to a school was when their daughter started dancing. An idle well-meaning offer of backstage assistance had often resulted in years of unstinting invaluable service, usually unpaid; making costumes, doing accounts, making coffee, staunching the wounds of the injured and the damaged egos of the principals. There were, she supposed, legions of these wonderful people – the length and breadth of the country – paying again and again in other kind for their children's dancing lessons, and rewarded again and again by being involved with the productions and achievements of the school, becoming invaluable and then, Lara knew with a shock, seemingly indispensable.

Perhaps, Miss Streete thought, as she curled her feet underneath her on the sofa, and took into her hands her cup and saucer of Earl Grey tea, perhaps it's time to hang up the shoes, pull down the curtain and call it a day.

And then she thought that if there was to be an end to it all, the school would certainly not expire with a whimper but with a bang. This, after all, was show biz! and she grinned at the portentousness of her thoughts. She'd always wanted to use that wonderful music of Prokofiev's *Cinderella*.

She got up from the sofa, ignoring the oh-so-familiar wrenching feeling in her left knee and searched for the tape, and put it into the machine and started the music flowing. How rich those bass lines, she thought; and the familiar translation of music into pattern painted shapes inside her head. Her thoughts were interrupted by the ring of the phone bell – quite in the wrong key. She turned the tape off angrily, cross at being interrupted, cross at the sequence of events that had made today so horrid.

It was her old friend Trudi. She was relieved, and she let go. And as she had done so many times in the past, Trudi listened and fielded the remarks.

``But they're not indispensable,'' she said.

``But they've been with me so long,'' Lara complained. ``I rely on them – they know the ways of the school – my ways.''

``Lara,'' Trudi said, ``the dancing school is *you* – you're the one that can't be replaced – only you can teach what you teach and the way you teach it. I happen to think – no, I know – as do countless people – that you have a very special gift.''

``But I can't do it without support,'' moaned Lara.

``Darling, the only real support you need is music and a pupil,'' Trudi interrupted.

``Well, I haven't many of them at the moment,'' continued Lara. ``They all seem to be fading away like the morning dew.''

``That's inevitable; these things have their seasons,'' Trudi reasoned.

``Well, it's winter here then,'' grumbled Lara.

``I bet,'' said Trudi sagely, ``that there's at least one pupil in your school that needs you as her teacher.''

And before she could stop herself, Lara thought of Claire Wells, saw her solemn little face, remembered how she had moved through a perfect *chassé* into a perfect *attitude à terre* only that morning, knew the pathos and excitement she would bring to the part of Cinderella.

Trudi attacked the silence. `` – Isn't there?'' she insisted.

``Yes . . . yes,'' said Lara.

``And you didn't start the school with Clara, or Jenny, or Annabel, or any of the people who help you now.''

``But they've all helped to make it what it is now.''

``So it will change – that's healthy,'' Trudi went on, and then heard her friend sniffle and knew what few people saw, that under Miss Streete's well-rehearsed role of authority there was someone who, so often, doubted herself – even in the face of tangible evidence. She laughed. ``Anyway – I know it's a hiccup – you'll manage.''

``Mm –'' Lara conceded ``s'pose so.''

``Anyway, I've rung with some wonderful news.''

``Oh, what?'' Lara asked.

``I'm going to be a granny.''

``Oh, wonderful, Trudi! When?''

``Next autumn.''

``Goodness me – what would you like?''

``A girl of course; Imo's set on it.''

``Oh well, let's hope she's not disappointed – would you be?''

``No, of course not, as long as it's healthy.''

And they chatted on for a while and then Lara replaced the phone and went back to the tape machine and let Prokofiev spill out over the carpet and wash away the shadows of sadness and disappointment.

Not for the first time, she wondered how her life might have been changed by marriage and children. She knew many dance teachers could only manage to run their schools simply because they were subsidised, as it were, by their husbands; and she knew of teachers whose schools became family concerns, husbands and sons operating lights and curtains at performances, daughters who acquired the appropriate qualifications to help their mothers. She had to admit there was something enviable about the cosiness of that kind of set-up. But her operation was her own – all her own it was, she realised, with a dull shock: her baby. She was damned if she would let it die. True, she'd have to contract – like one of those huge red stars that gently imploded but became, she knew, not only very small but oh, so very bright.

And Trudi was right – Claire Wells and all the other Claire Wellses needed what she arrogantly conceded only she could give her. As did Claire's mother; she had trusted her burgeoning baby ballerina to Miss Streete; this was Lara's burden and privilege – and this was the trembling living thing she gave to the world – unwrapping the larva, releasing the butterfly.

The mystical veiled melody that belonged to the Fairy Godmother gave way to the sudden mad joyous burst of music that belonged to the Fairy of Spring. ``Run, run, *pas de chat, sissone, sissone* . . . and *pointe fondu* . . .'' Lara found herself saying, feet pattering on the carpet, hands fluttering, and then remarked, as if startled by a sudden truth, ``That's all I *can* do . . . dance.''